A Quirk of Fate

A Quirk of Fate

by
Tallman (Tolly) Oskar
(the pseudonym)

DORRANCE PUBLISHING CO., INC.
PITTSBURGH, PENNSYLVANIA 15222

ISBN # 0-8059-6410-X
Printed in the United States of America

First Printing

For information or to order additional books, please write:
Dorrance Publishing Co., Inc.
701 Smithfield Street
Third Floor
Pittsburgh, Pennsylvania 15222-3906
U.S.A.
1-800-788-7654
Or visit our web site and on-line catalog at www.dorrancepublishing.com

Acknowledgments

I want to thank two of my daughters for all their help, Jean Beck and Edith Montgrand. As we reflect back and remember all the good laughs, we know we've gained a wealth of experience.

How Tallman (Tolly) Oskar Came to Exist

We were blessed with five children that we are extremely proud of,
and we are equally proud of their spouses and descendants.
With the arrival of our fourth child, we had a family of four
and none of them old enough to go to school.
In the rural area of "Sask" that we chose to make our home,
there was no electricity, no running water,
and disposable diapers had yet to be invented.
In election years, those seeking to replace the current government
had a slogan, "It's time for a change."
For their information it was always time for a change at our house.
It should also be noted that there was no kindergarten in those
years, nor was there much opportunity to make friends
with children of other families.
They did however play (and fight) well together.
And as many children will do they created an invisible playmate
to join in their games, though, at times the friend became real,
as one of them played the part of "Tolly Oskar."
The legs of the blue jeans I would buy were always too long,
My wife would cut them off, then hem the pant legs.
And it was the cut-off circle of denim that became a hat for
Tolly Oskar.

So when choosing a pseudonym to write under it would seem
Tolly Oskar was an apt choice
(though Tallman for the abbreviated Tolly was my idea).

Chapter 1

Williston, North Dakota, 1969

Doris Aimes sat toying with her pencil while a career counselor spoke to the graduating class. She was only half listening, as she had all but settled on enrolling in a course as a dental assistant, one of the many courses offered at the Technical School in Williston. Oh, she had given token consideration to a few of the other careers, but had quickly discarded the ideas.

It did not take much thought to skip over some. There was nursing, they had some pretty dirty jobs to do, long hours and shift work, at least at the beginning. Teaching might be okay, but the market was already flooded with teachers. Doris knew of people who had studied to become teachers and they were now working as waiters and waitresses.

Gifted with a natural ability to learn, Doris had always enjoyed school. Her parents were affluent enough to pay for any post-secondary education she chose. She would, of course, have to make the right choice, but a dental assistant seemed to her as something she would enjoy.

One career she did not want, at least not yet, was the one her sister Laura had chosen. Laura was Doris' older sister by seven years, and had married right out of high school. Since their marriage six years ago, Laura and her husband, Ben, had been blessed with three children and were expecting a fourth. Ben was good to Laura and they seemed happy in their cozy bungalow in Dayton, Ohio. Nonetheless, Doris could not picture herself in her sister's role.

Doris had a bit of encouragement as she considered the role of dental assistant. One of her friends had graduated from that same course a couple of years ago, she now had a full time position working nine to five, Monday through Friday.

1

She had already checked the entrance requirements for the program. They were a high school diploma with a minimum grade average of 60 percent, biology 50 percent, and one additional science. Applicants must be in possession of a CPR level C and a Standard First Aid Certificate prior to commencement of the two year program. Good medical and dental health were recommended for all applicants. Doris easily met the requirements, so she proceeded to enroll in the CPR/First Aid course.

Jack Nelson had been dating Doris for over a year now, Jack would be her escort for graduation. Jack was a nice guy, three years her senior. Doris had known him for as long as she could remember and they were comfortable together.

Jack Nelson had had an unhappy childhood. His father Einar Nelson died when Jack was seven. Two years later his mother, Sophia remarried, a man named Gunder Olafson. Jack and his stepfather never got along, Jack was considered a burden who was always in the way. Consequently, Jack shouldered the blame for anything and everything that happened to go wrong. Gunder would ridicule him for his poor grades at school. Once in a spelling exam Jack got a mark of 68 percent, which was the second highest in his class, but rather than give any words of encouragement, all the old stepdad offered was "the rest of the class must not be very bright."

Sophia was a timid little mouse, who could never stand up to her new husband. As a result, Jack continued to endure the abuse.

In 1959 twin boys were born to Sophia and Gunder. Jack was secretly pleased with the news thinking this would relieve some of his stepfather's resentment towards him and also provide him with some friends when his half-brothers got older. However, with a ten year age spread the closeness Jack craved with his brothers never materialized. Jack was an adult for as long as the twins could remember.

Before the twins were a year old, their father disappeared. He left no note of goodbye. His clothes were gone and the bank account emptied. All of this took place when Jack's mother was at a parent-teacher interview to discuss Jack's poor grades. The following day the police were notified of Gunder's disappearance and a missing person notice was filed. The family never heard of him again and Jack never shed any tears over the loss.

After the stepdad left, times were tough financially. Jack was eleven years old and managed to get a part-time job delivering groceries after school. He didn't earn much and what he did bring home went to help pay the household bills. At such a young age Jack wore his responsibilities like a cloak and inwardly thought, *Better than when that old man was around.* Sophia took jobs cleaning houses, which wasn't easy as she had to take the twins with her, but somehow they survived.

Jack, as has been noted, never excelled at school, so he dropped out as soon as he reached his sixteenth birthday, as the law did not require him to continue any longer. He liked working with his hands and once he was out of school he got a job at a local garage. He pumped gas, changed tires, and handled other small jobs that came along.

Eight years had passed since Jack's stepfather walked out of their lives. The war in Vietnam had been raging for four years. Prior to the United States government announcing to the world that they would send American troops to protect the South Vietnamese against the Russian supported Viet Cong, probably 80 percent of Americans had never heard of Vietnam. There were also suggestions that the protection wasn't as much for the Vietnamese, as it was for American investments in the country. Who knew what it was all about?

For some time now Americans of Jack's age were being drafted into the military to serve in Vietnam. Jack had received one call but the draft board granted a temporary exemption on compassionate grounds, as he was the sole supporter of his mother and twin brothers. Jack had heard of other men in his position who managed to get an exemption on compassionate grounds only to be called up later. It seemed everyone had to do a tour of duty, and after a reasonable amount of time, the military expected those exempted to have made arrangements that would take care of any commitments.

The news was full of reports of protest groups proclaiming the war in Vietnam senseless, unnecessary, and a waste of young American lives, as well as taxpayers' money. Jack even considered joining one of these groups, but thought better of it, coming to the conclusion that it would be pointless. They had been protesting now for at least three years, and the government showed no inclination or intentions of withdrawing from Vietnam. Besides all that ever came of the protest marches was a few young people ending up in jail or being injured. Jack suspected the media focused in on the worst cases of police brutality, like when they would show some long haired kid getting beaten over the head with a truncheon. He guessed that was the type of journalism that sold. No! Jack would not travel to one of the larger centers just to join a protest group.

There were a lot of young Americans leaving the States and crossing the border into Canada to avoid the draft. They considered themselves conscientious objectors. Who knows what these objectors did once they entered Canada, or what would happen if they tried to return home. Would they have to forfeit their American citizenship? Strange the thoughts that traveled through one's mind to justify avoidance of duty. Duty! It was his duty to look after his mother, provide food for his brothers, and now it was his duty to go to some country he didn't know existed. He was to protect people he had never heard of from an enemy that was equally unheard of. Yes indeed, Jack was sick of duty!

Jack's thoughts returned to Doris Aimes. Doris had blossomed into a real beauty in the last year or so. They had never discussed anything as serious as matrimony, but there was an unspoken understanding as far as Jack was concerned.

Doris was talking of taking a course at the local Technical School. Jack wondered if she could take the same course anywhere. She was clever enough. If she would marry him, maybe they could both go to Canada. That might be an option. Doris was smart, and Jack wasn't afraid of hard work. They could have a good life together. There was of course Jack's mother to think of, but if he was sent to Vietnam he wouldn't be around anyway. He might even be killed, for God's sake.

After the graduation dance in June, Jack asked Doris Kathleen Aimes to be his wife. Doris said, "Jack, I love you, but I'm just not ready for marriage." She assured him there was no one else she was interested in, "It is just that I want to be self-reliant, I want to be independent, I want . . . I want . . . I don't want to be like my sister." She finally blurted out, "I have been accepted into the Dental Assistant's course, it takes two years to complete. Once I have my diploma, we'll talk again of marriage, all right," she pleaded. They

4

would surely have a better chance at a quality of life with two incomes, she reasoned. As far as the draft went, there were now news reports that the Viet Cong were being driven back. Maybe Jack would not be called to serve his country. Maybe.

Chapter 2

Tudor, Saskatchewan, 1979

Late in the nineteenth century, a railroad was being constructed across Canada that would connect the Atlantic and Pacific oceans. As the rail line made its way across the Canadian prairies, towns sprang up in its wake like mushrooms. It was one of these towns-to-be that saw the arrival of a wealthy gentleman from England by the name of J. Percival Holmes. Since he was wealthy and came from England, the locals assumed he must be a lord. The result of the assumption was that he became known as "Lord Percy," even though he had never been a member of the British House of Lords.

It was what he did on arrival that gave the potential town its name. He built a mansion on the corner of a street junction that became Railway Avenue and Main Street. He predicted that when they were given Provincial status, their town would be the seat of Government, and he would be the first Premier. Neither prediction came to be, but his mansion stood out like an emerald, among the tents and sod shacks that were springing up. On hearing of it, people came from miles away, just to see such an edifice in all its grandeur.

It was a two story structure, with a spiral staircase to the upper level. The floors were all hardwood, except for the flagstone in the kitchen. Tapestries and paintings graced the walls; beautiful carpets were laid in all the bedrooms, as well as the parlor. Some thought the carpets came from Persia, Lord Percy never said. Double doors of oak, were installed on the side facing Main Street. Few had ever seen anything like it, and wondered why two doors were needed for entrance to the front room. Wouldn't it make the place harder to heat? They found out when the elaborate furnishings arrived, as both doors had to be open to let the various items pass through.

It was the two door mansion that was to give the town its name.

The address of anyone living there was Tudor, Northwest Territories, until 1905 when the Province was formed, changing it to Tudor, Saskatchewan.

It was in this small town of Tudor that Harry Welks was born. The year was 1949. Babies born during the buoyant years following the second world war were known as "baby boomers." Tudor now had a population of one hundred sixty four and was a twenty minute drive on a paved highway east of Moose Jaw. Harry was popular, both as a kid and now as a young adult. His parents, Frank and Betty Welks were good community people, but never had a lot of money. Frank's job as the postmaster in Tudor paid enough for a comfortable living, but not really enough to set anything aside. There was no high school in Tudor, so when it came to sending Harry to grade nine in Moose Jaw, they were glad to see the formation of the larger school district, and the provision of school bus service from Tudor into Moose Jaw. If Frank had had to pay for Harry's accommodation as well as tuition for four years of high school, it was unlikely he would have been able to do it.

The budget was strained enough when they paid for a hairdressing course for Mildred, their only daughter. Mildred was two years older than Harry, and it was through the good graces of some people they knew in Moose Jaw who gave her a place to live, in exchange for helping around the house in her spare time. After completing the hairdressing course Mildred was able to get a job in a local beauty parlor. About a year later she married an airman, who was stationed at the Canadian Forces Base in Moose Jaw.

Mildred's husband was just beginning his military career when they met and married in a simple ceremony in Moose Jaw. They lived in the married quarters on the air base, which fit their budget nicely. Bob was ambitious and wanted to move up the ladder quickly, so he took advantage of every course available, from technical to leadership. At the same time Mildred continued her hairdressing trade, adding to her clientele from new acquaintances on the base. After two years Mildred's husband received his well deserved promotion and was subsequently transferred to Camp Borden in Ontario. It was a bittersweet time for Mildred as she would be leaving her job, her friends, and her family behind; however, she was happy for her husband and happy to think that they would soon be able to start their own family.

◆ ◆ ◆

On completion of grade twelve with better than average marks, Harry started thinking about his future. He liked working with numbers and was good at it, as a matter of fact his favorite subject in school was mathematics. Could he become a chartered accountant? It would mean going to a university, and that would cost money.

There was a government student loan program available, and on looking into it seemed he would qualify. However two things happened in Harry's life that put an end to any ideas of going to university.

Harry's dad, Frank Welks, was born in 1918, and grew into an adult during those terrible depression years of the 1930s. He became part of a group of young men that scoured the country looking for work. Many of these young men chose freight trains as a means of transportation during their search for employment, it was referred to as "riding the rods." The practice was illegal but nothing much was done about it, there were literally thousands of these young men. There were several terms to describe them, they were sometimes called "Knights of the Road" or "Railroad Bums," but life for Frank went on, and at times he did get a job for a while at one thing or another, until the outbreak of World War Two. It was then that much changed for the Knights of the Road. Many of them enlisted in the armed forces, and found themselves back on the trains again. This time they were in the passenger cars, riding on cushions at the expense of the federal government, as they were posted from one training camp to another.

Frank enlisted with the "Princess Patricia Light Infantry Dragoons," better known as the "Piddle-D-Gees" in September of 1939, and was posted overseas in 1940, he wasn't to see Canada again until 1945. During those years he surely saw more than his fair share of the action.

On his return to Tudor, Saskatchewan, the local post office had no one to run it, so he applied for and got the job. The job was pretty well a sure thing from the start, because the postal service was under the jurisdiction of the government, so most any job they had to offer went to a returned soldier, as long as the applicant met the requirements. Frank was a returned man, and besides that he was the only one that applied for the job.

Frank Welks settled down to become one of Tudor's solid citizens, he bought a house and a lot, and the next year he married Betty McIsaac, a local girl that he had known since childhood. As we have already noted two children were born to them, Mildred and Harry.

The first thing to happen that would change the life of Harry Welks was a letter his dad got inviting him to a reunion of his old regiment. The reunion would be in Calgary in July, there was a nominal registration fee that was to accompany his intention to attend. Frank sent the needed fee by return mail, then started to make arrangements for holidays that would coincide with the reunion dates. From then on all he could talk about was meeting his old friends from the army and being able to introduce Betty to them.

Betty wasn't nearly as enthused as her husband about the reunion. She was sure that she would be bored to tears as she listened to war stories that she knew nothing about, to say nothing of having to put up with the tobacco smoke and whiskey fumes for three days. They had planned a trip to eastern Canada that summer to see their newborn granddaughter, but as Frank said, the reunion was a one-time occasion, while the new baby would still be there the next year. He justified his reasoning by saying that they would enjoy the grandbaby much more when she was a year older and able to do more things. Reluctantly Betty agreed to the Calgary trip, mainly because she couldn't bring herself to do anything to dampen Frank's enthusiasm.

A good portion of the Trans-Canada Highway is divided double lane highway, but there are a few stretches that are not yet completed. Such a stretch existed near the west side of the Province of Saskatchewan and it was on one of those stretches that Frank and Betty Welks met their tragic death. Frank did most of his driving on the Regina to Moose Jaw portion, where the road was divided into two lanes, so the traffic was all going one way. It was the general theory that Frank forgot about there being two-way traffic.

It was when he had pulled out to pass a motor home that he was hit head-on by a big truck. Frank and Betty were both killed instantly, while the truck driver was unhurt. What a cruel twist of fate, after all those years in the thick of battle and never getting as much as a scratch, then to lose his life when en route to relive those war years with his old buddies. Indirectly Frank Welks lost his life as a result of the war.

The other thing that brought about a change in Harry's life was a dance at the town hall in Tudor. It happened this way; a local girl by the name of Lucille Harper had asked him if he was going to take in the dance. He said, "Oh! I haven't really thought about it." "Well 'The Rhythm Pals' are playing, and they have a new piano player that they say is really good." She continued on by saying that it would be nice to go and hear them. Harry knew that what she really meant was, "Will you be my escort?" Harry had never given Lucille much thought, *Oh, she was okay,* he guessed, *and anyway what's to lose.* So when he asked her if she'd like to go with him, she quickly accepted.

Dance night soon arrived, and Harry and Lucille were on hand when the band started playing the first number. They naturally paired off for the first dance, when it ended Harry was prepared to take Lucille back to a seat at the table, where they had joined some of their friends as they entered the hall.

Lucille, however, had other ideas as the band started playing again. She clung to Harry, saying, "Hey! This is a waltz, I just love waltz music, don't you?" So they again paired off, and it was Lucille that was the bold one as she snuggled up cheek to cheek, to the tune of "The Tennessee Waltz."

Harry didn't really want to become involved with any girl to the point where they would become, "Well, an item." However, as she cuddled closer and closer, Harry thought, *What the heck, if we're going to become an item of kitchen table conversation, we might as well make it worthwhile.* So when he made the suggestion about it getting pretty hot in here, and said, "Could I get us a couple of cokes and take them to the car to drink?" Lucille was quite agreeable to the idea. The token resistance she offered in the back seat of the car, disappeared like butter melting on a hot roll.

♦ ♦ ♦

On learning of the death of his parents Harry's first move was to call his sister Mildred with the sad news. As he placed the call to Mildred in eastern Canada, he estimated the two hour time change would make it a little after five P.M. and she should be home from work.

A year after settling in at Camp Borden, Mildred gave birth to a beautiful healthy baby girl. They named her Annette and immediately called Mildred's parents in Saskatchewan with the happy news. Mildred couldn't wait for her parents to come for a visit and introduce them to their granddaughter. Little did she realize at the time how soon the feeling of euphoria would end with a phone call from her brother Harry.

Mildred answered on the first ring and, as was expected, she was left speechless at the news. However she was able to get herself together enough to talk of what needed to be done. Well she supposed it would only be right for them to come to the funeral, but gee! The airfare out and back would be quite a bit, she wasn't sure they could handle it. "Well! I'll tell you what, when Bob gets home we'll talk it over and I'll get back to you."

Because Frank Welks was a member of the Moose Jaw branch of The Royal Canadian Legion, the Legion helped with all the funeral arrangements. The estate of course would have to pay for it, but Frank had taken care of that matter himself by taking out an insurance policy years ago. At least that was one less worry.

Mildred called back that evening and said she didn't think they would be able to make it out for the funeral. She felt sure that Mom and Pop would understand their situation and the money for airfare could be put to better use some other place. They would, of course, call one of the florists in Moose Jaw and have a wreath delivered. To which Harry replied that he was sure something like that would be expected of them, even though there would no doubt be lots of sprays, wreaths, and so on that would show up from the many friends they had. Harry then went on to ask, "Would it be all right with you if we jointly bought a really good wreath to put on a stand right between the two caskets?" Mildred thought that would be good, as Harry would be in a position to select personally the right one. "Just let us know what we will owe you."

Then there seemed to be nothing more to say for a moment, but Mildred broke the silence, when she said, "This may not be the time to bring up the delicate subject of the estate, but I don't suppose Dad had a will, so I will likely have to sign some kind of a release that will let you inherit any assets there are. I just want you to know that I will be more than willing to do whatever had to be done." Harry thanked her and then went on to tell her that he was sure that their father had no will, and as to assets, about the only thing of any value would be the house and lot in Tudor. Other than that, there was only the car, and it was a total write-off, though there would likely be some money coming from the auto insurance for it. Mildred said, "Well, you will no doubt be able to use any available money that comes along, as there are sure to be some unexpected expenses you were not counting on."

"As to the house and lot, I don't expect real estate in Tudor is worth much, but if you continue to live there you will need a house. I'll admit to being a bit selfish here, as what I really want is to have you keep the house up, so that if we can get back West sometime I'll be able to show little Anne where I grew up."

"You will probably marry someone before long and you will have a nice home for the new Mrs. Welks. Is there any girl that has caught your eye yet?" And Harry said, "No, there isn't."

Little did either of them think that a girl named Lucille Harper would shortly be walking into Harry's life. Harry certainly couldn't know that an incident, in the back seat of a car, now all but forgotten, would come back to make a change that would alter the path that the rest of his life had been destined to follow.

Chapter 3

Williston, North Dakota, 1971

Time went on, for Jack Nelson and Doris Aimes. They continued dating and in 1971 Doris graduated as a dental assistant. It was at her graduation ceremony that Jack again asked Doris to be his wife. This time she accepted and wedding plans began to take shape.

Sophia was more than pleased as her son's relationship with Doris culminated at the highest level that a man and woman can reach. Jack deserved some happiness. Ever since her second marriage had ended the way it did, she had harbored a feeling a guilt, as she believed it was her life choices that had denied Jack a childhood.

While it was too late to undo anything that had already taken place, there still might be something she could do for her eldest son. Her thoughts turned to the city of Bismark and her brother-in-law Andrew Nelson who still lived there.

When Sophia's first husband Einar was still alive, they had kept in reasonably close touch with his brother Andrew and Mary, Andrew's wife. The distance between Williston and Bismark of course limited the number of times they actually were able to visit each other. Still they exchanged Christmas cards, as well as other letters throughout the year.

Sophia remembered well that first time she had the pleasure of meeting Mary. That was the year they made the trip to Bismark by rail, and spent three wonderful days that included Christmas, with Mary and Andrew. Jack was three years old then, and had so much fun, even though he was too young to remember much about it. His mother remembered the holiday quite well and the fuss Andrew and Mary made over Jack.

She guessed the reason for their taking to Jack to such an extent was the fact that they were unable to have children. Sophia felt sorry for them as she reflected on their problem. As Einar told her, Mary had become pregnant during their first year of marriage. It was after three days of agonizing labor that she had delivered a stillborn baby. Not only was there no baby to see grow up and to be proud of, but Mary had almost died during those terrible three days. Once the crisis was over and the doctor assured him Mary was out of danger, Andrew had a vasectomy. Never again would he see his Mary suffer like that.

She didn't remember a lot about the Bismark holdings, other than that the one bedroom house was well-kept and clean. On that occasion she had shared the only bed with Mary, with Jack snuggling down between them. The two men slept in the front room, one on the couch and the other on the floor. She knew it didn't matter much to the men, as they hardly slept anyway, being too busy talking. Their childhood in Norway, the trip to America, and life here since, all got a good going over on that visit.

Mary was not only a good housekeeper but an excellent cook as well. It was a lucky day for Andrew when he found her. Mary came from Ireland and was employed as domestic help in Bismark. Andrew, a plumber by trade, was called on to do a repair job in the home where Mary worked, and that's where the relationship began. Sophia just loved to hear Mary talk, that Irish lilt was so pleasing to the ear, almost like music. She knew her own Norwegian accented version of English must sound quite coarse to Mary, but then she was probably used to it by now, as Andrew's English was no better than her own.

It was the small acreage that Mary and Andrew lived on, near the outskirts of town, which turned Sophia's thoughts to Bismark. How nice it would be if Jack and Doris had something like that. Why, they could produce so much of their living, right on the land. It was much like the property they had in Norway, until their father had uprooted the family and they all moved to America. Actually as she now thought about it, life as she remembered it was good in Norway. It must have been all those glowing reports of the great opportunities America had to offer that had caused her dad to make the move.

It was the year that Jack turned seven that he got to go and spend two weeks of his summer holidays with the Bismark aunt and uncle. This time he made the trip by bus, and all by himself at that. His mother was naturally glad for him, and happy when he was safely home again. She wondered if he was exaggerating a bit when he told her about how hard they made him work. All he did was pull weeds in the garden, shell peas, and stuff. Sophia smiled a bit at this, and said, "Oh! Come now, you didn't work all the time. I heard that you went to a circus in Bismark one day Did you like that?" Then Jack told her about having a ride on the Ferris wheel, and how the other kids were so scared and screamed all the time. He sure wasn't scared, he liked it when he was at the top of the wheel and could see all over Bismark. When he got big, he would join a circus and operate one of those wheels, he could see how it was done.

"Did you like your Aunt Mary?" she asked. "Oh yes, she made the best sugar cookies, they were as big as the lid of a jam pail," said Jack. "But she sure has a funny way of talking Why does she talk like that?"

It was not long after Jack's visit to Bismark that she had lost her husband. Her in-laws came to Williston for Einar's funeral, and that was the last time she would ever see them. They did still keep in touch with their letters, though it was always Mary that did the writing, until two years ago that was. That was when Sophia got that telegram letting her know that Mary had passed away very suddenly of a heart attack. She naturally sent back a message of condolences, regretting that financial circumstances would prevent her from coming to the funeral. She didn't mention it in her reply, but just to buy a sprig of flowers was a real blow to their budget. When she wired the flowers from a Williston florist, she had the clerk add Einar's name to hers and her son's, as the card was filled out. Wondering as she did it, *if it were possible for Einar and Mary to have met in the next world. Perhaps they were talking about their time on earth, especially that wonderful Christmas when they were all together.*

Andrew continued to write to Sophia, though not to the extent that Mary had. It was a letter he had written last June that gave her the notion that there may still be something she could do for Jack. In his letter he told her he was now a resident of a nursing home in Bismark. Then he went on to say that he had been diagnosed with bone cancer. He still had his acreage outside of town, but would likely have to sell it. It would be difficult to part with, but the buildings would soon

15

deteriorate now that they were vacant. He didn't say much more about it, other than to mention that it would not make much difference what he got for it, as the nursing home would take from the sale proceeds for his keep till the money was gone.

Sophia decided that there were two situations here that would complement each other. If he hadn't already sold it, Jack and Doris could make it their future home. Andrew would have a buyer that surely he would be more happy about than if he had to sell to a total stranger.

Without saying anything to the young couple, she wrote to Andrew. As she put the words to paper, she wondered if it was the right thing to do. Would they think she was meddling? Nor did she really want Jack and her new daughter-in-law to leave Williston, knowing that such a move would limit the times she would be able to see them.

All these misgivings were pushed aside, however, as she thought of the increased opportunities a larger center like Bismark would have to offer. But foremost in her mind was the acreage, and the produce that would come off it. Why Jack might not even need to get a job. She remembered Andrew having a workshop out behind the house, and with Jack being so good with his hands, he could make all kinds of things that he could sell, such as bird houses, doll houses, and more.

With her mind made up, she wrote that his nephew Jack was now twenty-one and about to marry the lovely Doris Aimes, adding that he might remember the Aimes family. Doris' mother had been a Hunter, the second daughter of the late William Hercules Hunter. Bill Hunter had been a member of the senate during the Roosevelt administration.

Her letter then went on to ask about his holdings at Bismark, making mention of her hopes that it could become the future home of the newlyweds.

Sophia was happy with the response from Andrew. Andrew told her he was pleased that things were going well for Jack. Yes, he still owned the five acres just three miles outside of Bismark. A good portion of his letter went on to describe the layout, buildings in good shape, unlimited water supply, any couple could easily get half their

16

living right off the land. He would be pleased if Jack and his new bride could buy it, going on to say that he would like to sell cheap. If he could, he would just give it to the young couple, in order to keep it in the family. However there was a law that prevented him from doing this. He did not elaborate on what law he meant.

His letter then said he would have to advertise the property for sale through a public forum. He would keep the kids informed as to any bids that came in, then if they wished they could acquire it by matching the highest bid. They could either pay him right out, or go the mortgage route, in which case it would be a lending institutions that paid him, and would hold the title till the mortgage was paid off. Yes, he remembered old Bill Hunter, though he had never voted for him, or for that matter any Republican.

When Sophia showed Andrew's letter to the couple about to be married, their interest perked up right away. Their enthusiasm was piqued even more when a second letter from Andrew arrived with a hundred dollar bill in it. He said it was his wedding present to them, and wished it could be more. This letter told them he planned to rewrite his will, making them his sole beneficiary. He hoped there would be something left for them, at the time of his passing but after the "care home" took their cut every month, there might not be much left, he had added. He sure hoped they would be able to make the purchase, and when they got settled in he would appreciate having them call on him.

Doris' mother filled them in on the law that required Andrew to advertise his holding for sale through a public forum. She remembered when the state had brought in the legislation. Her dad, old grandfather Hunter was in the senate at the time.

The legislation came about because people that knew their next move was to a care home would dispossess themselves by giving their assets away, usually to family members. Then when they arrived at the care facility destitute, they became wards of the taxpayers. To prevent this the state legislature had passed a law that would require a person going to any of these facilities to publicly advertise for sale any assets they wished to dispose of. Any family member could then match the highest bid, should they want whatever the asset might be. The law would not affect items that had been already disposed of if the transaction had taken place at least three years prior to the individual entering the care facility. The three year time factor was written in because it would be unlikely that anyone would plan for their entry into a care home, any more than three years in advance.

Once Andrew advised them of the bid they would have to match, they were not long in making up their mind to buy. Doris' dad did suggest that Andrew's story of changing his will, sounded a bit like a carrot on a stick that would encourage them to buy his place.

Doris' parents gave them a thousand dollars as a wedding present to be used as a down payment. It took awhile to arrange the mortgage, but they finally bought the good uncle's acreage sight unseen. Well, not quite sight unseen. Sophia was able to relate as much as she could remember from that visit almost twenty years ago. Jack still had a vague memory of his visit when he was seven.

Jack and Doris were married on New Year's Day, 1972. They took a two day honeymoon trip to Winnipeg, Canada. They promised each other that when they were established and had enough money, they would take a more elaborate trip. They had heard about Winnipeg having built a new casino like the ones in Las Vegas. Since neither of them had ever been to Las Vegas, they didn't know what to expect. They also wondered if they would see any "draft dodgers." Of course they wouldn't know what one of them looked like either.

While they couldn't bring themselves to actually put money in the machines, they were quite impressed as they watched other people. The clatter of coins falling into the tray in front of a player was enough to excite anyone. Jack, with a natural interest in anything mechanical, couldn't figure out just how they must work. One in particular had the face of a money on each reel, if one or more monkeys stopped on the horizontal line of the display window some coins would fall to the tray below while the monkey or monkeys would chatter and dance around, right on the reel.

On one occasion they watched a lady playing. The newlyweds thought she must have unlimited resources, as she handed out twenty-dollar bills to a young girl with a cart that had piles of coins, all done up in paper rolls. Doris noted she got two of the rolls for twenty dollars, when the roll was struck against the holding tray, out came a bunch of quarters, and into a slot on the machine they disappeared. Jack and Doris could see that a lot more coins went into the machine than ever fell into the tray below. Jack asked her if she ever got a real big payout, she replied, "Not very often, but this is the one place that you can forget all your other troubles and concentrate only on beating that damn machine."

With that they left her, as they wondered, *Wouldn't your other troubles be just that much worse, if you lost a bundle of money while trying to beat the machine?*

From there they went to the casino restaurant, where a buffet dinner was available, so much food, it was unbelievable, so much to choose from, take as much as you want, the sign said. The cost was a mere $2.99. They couldn't believe it, in addition to that, when they changed their American currency to Canadian, they received an extra ten cents for each dollar.

They made the mistake of piling their plates too high with the various selections of salads, chicken or fish cuts, etc. as they went along the buffet counter. At the end of the line, there are two men with chef's hats and white smocks, one carving a baron of beef roast, the other cutting a baked ham, but with plates already holding more than they could eat, it was a very small cut of either main meat course that got laid on top. Next time they would be more selective as they filled their plate.

On their return home, they told each other that it had been a good honeymoon, as well as an interesting experience. After spending one night in Williston at the home of Doris' parents, their possessions were loaded into Jack's three year old Ford half-ton truck. Then after the hugs and kisses, and good luck wishes, it was off to Bismark and their new home.

Chapter 4

Bismark, North Dakota, 1972

The newlywed Nelsons followed the directions from Bismark out to their new home. Driving into the yard they were quite pleased with what they saw. The buildings looked as if they could have been painted sometime in the last few years, perhaps no more than five or six. The house was white with green trim, while the outbuildings were red with white trim. Even though it was winter Doris could visualize where she could have flowers, where the vegetable garden would be and so on.

On entering the house, however, they really got the shock of their lives. The place was absolutely overrun with mice, there was chewed-up paper and other material, mixed with their droppings everywhere. The walls were beaver-board, a paper product that was widely used when the house was built, probably sometime in the 1920s. Being paper, the walls were a haven for mice, they had riddled it with holes, for no more reason than to get to the other side. If the wallboard itself wasn't enough of a playground for them, there was the added incentive of the wood shavings that had been used as insulation, they were spilling out through the holes, to contribute to the debris that all but covered the floor.

At first Doris was simply speechless, and not only that, she felt nauseated and thought she would throw up The stale animal that permeated the place was just as objectionable as the sight that met their eyes. The smell was alleviated to some extent as they opened windows, and left both the front and back doors open. When Doris finally regained control of herself, her first words were "We'll have to go to a motel, there is no way we could go to bed in this mess."

While Jack didn't disagree with her outright, he did start thinking of some way around the problem, so he said, "Not exactly as we had it pictured is it. To go to a motel is going to take money. Money that could be used for the renovating we are going to have to do. Already I can see a good chunk of money going out, as we are going to have to clear out all this old beaver-board and replace it with gyprock, and use good rock wool insulation."

Then he added, "And you know, as far as staying here, we may as well try and make the best of it. Once I start cleaning some this debris out, it's unlikely that the mice will bother us as long as I keep working at it." Doris was still not convinced, as she went on to say, "But even if there were no mice, just look how dirty that bed is, surely you don't expect us to sleep in that."

Jack still didn't want to go to a motel. He had two reasons for not wanting to go, one thing, of course, was the cost, and the other reason was that the only way to get the place in shape was to get at it, something he wouldn't be able to do from a motel. So he said to Doris, "Look, honey, the wedding gifts were given to us to use, so why not start now? I think I remember seeing a set of sheets and pillow cases, if you put them on the bed at least the bedding next to us would be clean." So after some thought Doris agreed to try it for one night, adding that there was a new blanket among the gifts as well as the sheets. They would have to leave the lights on, as she was sure she would never fall asleep anyway, not even for a second.

They had picked up a pizza and a quart of milk, so they had the making of what was to be their first meal in their new home. Jack then went to work, stripping the front room of its interior wallboard and just throwing the stuff in a pile beside the front step. He would sooner have been able to load it into his truck as he went, but they were not about to unload their possessions until some degree of order was made in what was to be their new home. Doris helped Jack as much as she could, but really this kind of work was not exactly a job that she'd had any training in.

By ten o'clock she told Jack her hands were getting sore, and so was her back. Jack said, "You had best lay off for now, I'll try to get the mess out of this room, and in the morning we can go to Bismark for breakfast, then we'll go shopping." So with that Jack carried in their overnight bag, and looked through their stuff till he found the bedding they were going to need. Doris made up the bed, and with that done she was glad to lie down, even though she was sure she would not go to sleep.

Jack continued working until well after midnight, and by then the front room was completely gutted. It made quite a pile beside the step, he would move it a bit further away when he would then burn it. It would not have to be moved far, as there was a light covering of snow on the ground that would prevent a fire getting out of control. A couple of times Doris pleaded with him to quit for the night and come to bed, but he would reply, "But just think, honey, at least the mice are being quiet."

Next morning Jack was up early and measured all the rooms, writing down each measurement as he went. He would leave it to a person at the lumber yard to do the calculation and tell him what he needed by way of material.

It only took Doris a few minutes to get ready for town, then it was into the truck and they were on their way. Doris had already sent job applications to two dental clinics in Bismark. The original plans had been to wait a week or two before either of them tried to get a job, but now with this unexpected expense of fixing the house, well, they would have to have some income. Doris and Jack now had a whole list of things to do, but first, they would go to a restaurant and have some breakfast.

The customers that had been ahead of them had left a copy of the daily paper in the booth. After the waitress took their order, Doris picked up the paper and started to scan the ads. As she did this, Jack said, "I hope you see one that's got a heck of a sale on gyprock, or maybe somebody has a milk cow for sale." Uncle Andrew had suggested they try to keep some livestock as the acreage had ample grass to carry them.

What Doris did see was that somebody had kittens to give away to any one that would give them a good home. On reading the ad, Doris said, "Do you think a kitten might discourage the mice as well as make a good companion." Jack replied, "By all means, and if it's here in Bismark we had better try and make a call before we go home." So that was agreed on, they would shop for a kitten, and the waitress was at their table with breakfast.

Well sated, Doris started making calls to the dental clinics where she had submitted her résumés. They had two reasons for Doris being the one to land a job first, she probably had the best chance of getting a job, and she would likely bring home a better paycheck. With his limited education they reasoned that if Jack would get a job, it would be at minimum wage. Further to that, Jack would have to be there if they were ever going to make the old house fit to live in.

Doris was lucky on her first call, the clinic had an opening and she could start the next day. This wouldn't leave much time to settle in, but they had better take it as they would soon be desperate to have enough money for groceries. With groceries in mind, the next stop was at a mall where Doris could buy the essentials while Jack went shopping for building materials.

The first lumber yard he stopped at could supply him with all he was going to need, but it would take more than one trip. The truck, as we remember, was still loaded with all their worldly possessions. All he could take on that trip were the insulation batts. When he had them piled on top of the already loaded truck, he bought about fifty feet of light rope to tie them down. Oh well, the rope would come in useful sometime.

Then it was back to the mall to pick up Doris and the groceries, Jack hoped her purchases were minimal, as about the only room left was in the cab of the truck. The two boxes that she had fit nicely between them on the seat.

The next decision to make was whether or not to follow up on the ad they had seen about kittens. The address took them to a modest home in the suburbs. The door was answered by a lady that looked to be in her sixties but who was dressed like a teenager. She was wearing a white ribbed-cotton halter top, with black jeans, leaving a good portion of her midriff bare. She was barefooted, showing her toenails that were painted the same sick purple as her fingernails. The doodads that danged from her ears looked like something that belonged on a Christmas tree. They were likely supposed to be a match for the double chain of beads that hung from her neck. Doris wondered what kind of a creature this was, as she noticed the makeup, and false eyelashes. She would soon find out that the lady's attire was only one sample of her strange mentality.

In answer to Jack's question about the ad; yes, she had four kittens that she would like to see go to a good home. They weren't so sure they wanted to take all four of them. *Goodness,* thought Jack, *that many could be as bad as having the mice.* But when they tried to explain that one of the kittens was all they really wanted, the lady said, "Oh, but they should be kept together, it would be just like breaking up a family of children to separate them, you know." This got Jack to thinking of an angle to use on the good lady, she must have the mother of the kittens around somewhere, and an adult would be a much better mouser than the kittens. "Have the kittens been weaned already and are they used to solid food?" asked Jack. "Oh, yes, Mistress hasn't nursed them now for almost two weeks and they are doing quite well," said the lady. This was when Jack came on with his convincing argument by saying, "As you just said, it would be upsetting to the kittens to be separated from each other, so wouldn't it be just as upsetting to be taken to new surroundings without their mother? They would be so lost, just like children on their first day of kindergarten are when there is no one around that they know. I am just wondering if you would considering loaning us Mistress, you did call her that I believe, for maybe a week, so the kittens can get settled in." As they talked Doris thought *Gee! Now we know the name of the cat, but we don't know the name of this old girl.* The lady thought a while and then said, "Well, as it happens I am going to be away for a week, and I was planning to put her in a boarding kennel, but maybe it would be okay if you kept her with her little family."

She then went on to explain the way in which Mistress was used to being looked after. She was to be fed only Purina Cat Mix, definitely no table scraps, Jack never said anything but thought she's probably relish a nice fresh mouse. Then the old girl rambled on about the toys she would send along, as Mistress played with her toys every day. There was a rubber ball, a wooden archway with a tennis ball suspended, and there was a rubber mouse. Jack had to smile a bit when she said that, as he thought, *Mistress, you will not be needing a rubber mouse.* Then she told them about a VCR tape that Mistress liked to watch, "Oh! You do have a TV and VCR, don't you?" When Jack told her they only had a TV she said she could let them have her VCR to use along with the tape that Mistress liked so well. "You see, the tape shows a cat walking across the keyboard of a piano, then jumping to

24

the top of it, across the top and back down, to go across the keyboard again. The tape is spliced so that it just shows the picture over and over again, and all the time the cat is saying 'meow, meow, meow' with the tempo rising and falling to the tune of 'Rock-a-bye-baby.' Oh! Mistress just loves it, she'll sit for hours at a time, just purring away as she watches."

Jack and Doris were both starting to wonder if this old dear was maybe a few bricks short of a full load, but they didn't comment. Instead, they told her they would be happy to look after Mistress in the manner that she was accustomed to. They added that they wouldn't have room for Mistress and her family on this trip, but were coming back to town right after lunch for more supplies, and if it was okay they would pick them up then. The good lady said that would be fine with her, she would have them ready to go.

On the way back to their home to be, Jack told Doris that the lifestyle Mistress was used to would likely change. "To start with," said Jack, "all feline species have a natural instinct to hunt, it just needs a bit of developing, and the way to do it is with hunger. One promise I'll be keeping is, she'll not get any table scraps, nor much of anything else for that matter. As for watching TV or playing with her toys she may not have time."

Chapter 5

Bismark, North Dakota

After leaving the cat lady, still thinking her a weirdo, and returning to the acreage they unloaded everything, and hoped that Mistress would be able to keep their stuff from being completely ruined. There was a limited amount of furniture, just essential pieces, there were no clothes closets just a few coat hooks beside a door that provided entry from the back porch to the kitchen. They put most of their clothes in a dresser, with a mirror, and the rest went into a chest of drawers that was part of the bedroom furnishings.

The kitchen boasted an electric stove, a fridge, and some built-in cupboards, with a sink cut into the countertop of the sideboard. There was also a wooden table and chair set that had been quite good in its day. In the cupboards, there were enough dishes and pots and pans to get by, and it would be more than adequate when their wedding gifts were added to the lot.

Once the truck was unloaded, Doris went into the groceries and got a can of soup and a loaf of bread, as well as some margarine. Before she prepared a lunch, she had Jack help her clean the kitchen as much as they could. That meant sweeping up the debris on the floor, as well as giving the table a scrubbing. After the chairs were wiped with a damp rag, Doris said it would have to do. By the time the soup was hot Doris had a few slices of toast ready, and thus they sat down to the second meal to be served in their new home.

With their lunch finished, Jack's next thought was to either find to make a crate that would be suitable for containing cats. In a shed just behind the house he found what he was looking for, it must have been a crate to haul chickens sometime or other. It would be just the thing to transport the kittens back to the acreage. Jack sure hoped that cat lady would approve of it. He thought that as long as the kittens were contained Doris could hold their mother on her lap, and everything should go well.

On returning to Bismark, Jack dropped Doris off at J.C. Penney's, as she said she should get some clothes that would be more suitable for the job of dental assistant than any that were in her wardrobe at present. At the clinic she had been told that a uniform was unnecessary, but neat serviceable garments would be appreciated. She would buy two white jackets, and two skirts, one dark blue and one grey, along with these she would need a pair of good walking shoes. She had enough blouses and stockings already, no need to select unnecessary any items. She was ready to go when Jack got back from the lumber yard. She told Jack about her purchases, saying she was really pleased with the items acquired, as well as the price paid.

Now it was time to pick up Mistress and her family. The good lady had them all ready to go, along with the VCR, the toys, and even part of a box of the special food Mistress was to have. No comment were made as the kittens were shut into the chicken crate and piled in the back of the truck, on top of the gyprock. Doris had not gotten out of the front seat, so Mistress was given to her to hold. The lady wished them luck, saying "I'll see you in a week." As they drove away Doris said, "Well now, that was quite a transaction, and all done without exchanging names."

Once home with no problems, the crate of kittens was carried into the shed that was just a bit south of the house. Before opening the crate, Jack scattered out some of the Purina cat food they'd been given, then went to the fridge and got the carton of milk that Doris had left there after her morning shopping. He found a discarded hub cap, and decided it would make a good cat dish, and left it near the crate with about a pint of milk in it. Then, after opening the crate, he went out of the door, closing it firmly behind him. The kittens would be left on their own for awhile.

Before starting to fit the insulation into the walls in the front room, Jack thought he should introduce Mistress to her new job. With the front room stripped bare there was no place for mice to take cover there. He would take a panel of beaver-board off a bedroom wall, then see how many mice would be scurrying about. Not only did three or four full grown ones come out, but also a mouse nest that was made up of chewed-up cloth and cotton, and nestled nicely into the wood shavings. In the nest were six baby nice, little pink ones with no hair. Mistress had not made any attempt to catch the adults as they ran about, but when Jack took her in his arms and pushed her nose into the nest of young ones, she just sniffed, and then quickly gobbled them up.

Doris thought that was so tragic. The poor little things never had a chance at life. "Oh! Come on, dear, be realistic. Those poor little things in two months time would have been big ones that would be digging, chewing, and destroying, making the mess that greeted us when we walked in here. Besides that, at two months they would be reproducing little pink things of their own. If we are going to make this place fit to live in, the mice have to go, pinks, greys, and the lot."

As it was still early afternoon Jack got right to it, and started installing the insulation batts in the front room. With Doris holding the batts in place, Jack quickly unfolded the paper edge on the batts and with the stapling gun, snapped in enough staples to hold them in place until the gyprock was nailed on. It went quite well and they soon had the two outside walls done. The interior walls, of course, needed no insulation.

The clock that had been given to them by Jack's former boss as a wedding gift now told them it was almost six o'clock, so Doris started to make their third meal in their new home. This time the fare would be a bit better. Among the groceries Doris had bought, were sausages, apples, carrots, and potatoes. With the apples peeled and boiled, she mashed them into applesauce. Their supper on the second evening, therefore, consisted of fried sausages, mashed potatoes, diced carrots, and applesauce, with a can of peaches for dessert. Jack complimented her on the meal, adding that, "It will be much better when summer in here. We can grow many of these vegetables ourselves."

While Doris was preparing supper, Jack measured and cut a number of sheets of gyprock to the right size. He would need Doris to hold each sheet in place until he could get a few nails in them. Once they were up he could finish nailing them by himself. Once again they worked well into the night, but before they stopped they were able to get all the dry-walling in the front room finished, even though there was a lot more nailing to do.

They were up and about by six the next morning. Doris took the truck to work, while Jack worked on the house. They agreed Doris would take a bag lunch to work as a measure of economy. What a difference for her. The home she grew up in didn't throw money away, but if they wanted something they just bought it without worrying about the cost. Much different from the Nelson home, where a nickel was never parted with until all the alternatives had been considered. Doris' lunch that day would be a bologna sandwich and an apple.

With Doris off to work after goodbye hugs and wishes for a good day, Jack went back to work on the restoration of the house. The first thing was to finish nailing the gyprock with sufficient nails to hold it in place until the end of time. Then it was time to mix the drywall compound with water, to make the "mud," until he brought it to the right consistency for easy application. Now with the trowel purchased at the lumber yard, he went to work filling the joints where the gyprock sheets joined each other, with the mixture of "mud," as it was called, and also applying a dab over each nailhead. Then it would have to be left to dry before it could be sanded down smooth enough to paint. After the first sanding, another coat of mud might have to be applied, then sanded again. Jack would not be satisfied until the job was done right.

While the mud was drying Jack decided to look around and get better acquainted with their acreage and the buildings. As he looked around, he realized that their dream home had been acquired without knowing much about it. Other than that holiday as a seven-year-old child, he'd really never even seen it. There were some things that went with it that he liked, the TV got adequate reception by means of a satellite dish, much better than a roof aerial that only brought in one or two stations.

As Andrew had said, there was an unlimited water supply, and everything connected with it was part of a system of its own, not dependent on any public or municipal service. That meant no water bills. The same thing applied to the sewage system. The only monthly billings would be from the company supplying electrical service, and from Ma Bell for telephone service. Before leaving Williston they had made arrangements to have these last two services transferred to their names.

The house, while on a good solid foundation, did not have a basement, it had a cellar that was just a hole in the ground about ten feet square and eight feet deep. Access to the cellar was from a trapdoor in the kitchen, with a permanent ladder descending to the floor of the excavation. On the floor was a cement slab about six feet square. The slab had two electric motors, complete with pumps on them. Jack had once helped a farmer north of Williston install a system much like this one. One of the pumps drew water from a sand point well, while the other activated the sewage system. He had seen the sewage discharge point about three hundred feet from the house, where the waste just disappeared into some trees. As long as it all worked the way it should, freezing was not a problem, any water still in the discharge line drained back to the septic tank when the sewage pump turned off.

The house was heated with propane gas. A thousand-gallon tank that contained the gas was located just a short distance east of the house. The tank was cradled in two concave cement blocks that were designed for that purpose. On reading the gauge on the tank Jack noted it was half full. He was glad to see that there would be no need to call a supplier for more gas until fall. The only appliance served by propane was a floor furnace in the front room, and once the weather got warm it wouldn't use any more fuel.

This heating system would keep one room warm, while the rest of the house would be somewhat cooler. *Well,* Jack thought, *here is something else to be left for another day, to install a real furnace with heating ducts to all the rooms.* One advantage of the floor furnace was that it made a good clothes dryer. Just hang the clothes on a clotheshorse and place it over the furnace. That's how Andrew must have done it because there was a clotheshorse in the porch.

Also in the porch was a Maytag washer. *A real antique,* thought Jack as he looked it over. It was powered by an electric motor that drove the machine's mechanism. There was no control switch. When it was plugged into an outlet it started, unplug it and it stopped. This applied to the agitator in the tub as well as the wringer mounted above the tub. To wring as much water out of the clothes as possible, the operator picked the items of clothing out of the tub and fed them into the rollers on the wringer. The water that was squeezed out just ran back into the tub. He must warn Doris to keep her hair done up inside a cap or something when using this thing More than one woman had had their hair torn out if she got a bit careless. It happened when an item was feeding into the wringer, and the operator let a lock of hair lay over the item that was feeding while reaching for another piece, and the hair got drawn in with it. He wouldn't want that to happen, as Doris had such beautiful long hair. He guessed it was those things that brought about the phrase "a tit in the wringer," referring to anyone that had got themselves in a jam.

There was no pump to draw water in or out. A length of garden hose was coiled up inside the tub. It was obvious that to fill the tub with water, either hot or cold, the hose needed to be connected to the desired tap at the kitchen sink. A rubber hose was permanently attached to the bottom of the tub. A clamp near the top of the tub held the hose above the water line and thus the water was contained in the tub. To drain it, you take the hose out of the clamp and lower it enough that the tub was emptied by gravity. The draining had been done, as Jack could see, by opening the back door, where a length of eaves-trough was nailed along the base of the porch till it reached the south-east corner of the building. With the drain hose laid in the trough the wash water ran out onto the ground at the corner. This would explain the absence of soap at the sewage discharge, but it must get smelly around the house in hot weather. Jack would try and get a piece of fire-hose or something, so that the wash-water would get carried further away. When they could afford it, this old antique would be replaced with a washer and dryer. There was getting to be quite a list of things to do later. Jack just hoped there would be enough "laters" to get them all done.

It seemed odd to Jack that Andrew still used such an obsolete method of washing clothes, and yet he had a TV dish, an item that had been on the market less than a year. The old boy must have liked TV.

For lunch Jack made himself a bowl of soup, from a can that was in one of the grocery boxes they had picked up the day before. After lunch the application of mud was dry enough to start sanding down. Sanding the walls is the most tedious job of all, as the work doesn't really make a noticeable showing, not like nailing up a sheet of wallboard. Anyway, with the sandpaper over the wood block he went to work, it was late afternoon when he finished all four walls. He then took a dry cloth and wiped away the accumulated dust, before applying another coat of mud. He was thankful to be able to leave it for awhile, and let this second application of mud dry.

As Doris would soon be home, he would surprise her by having supper started. All the perishable products that were bought the day before were now in the fridge. Among the fridge items was a small pork roast. On finding a suitable roaster, the meat went into the oven, after adding enough water to cover the bottom of the roaster pan. With this done he picked out a large carrot, an apple, and a small head of cabbage. These items he would grate, then mix them together along with some mayonnaise, plus a touch of mustard. Once the ingredients were well stirred he had a bowl of quite palatable coleslaw. Next he peeled some potatoes that would go into the roasting pan when the meat was partially cooked. He was pleased with his efforts, and decided to lie on the couch for a while. The couch, of course, had been moved into the kitchen for the renovations. He didn't intend to, but he fell asleep, and didn't hear Doris until she was in the house.

Doris was happy to see that supper was almost ready and told Jack she didn't realize he had that kind of culinary knowledge. As they ate their meal Doris told how her day had gone. She liked her boss and said the clients were all nice people. Some, realizing she was new, had asked where she came from. One in particular said he was sure he knew her dad. Jack was happy for her. Doris did the dishes while Jack went back to sanding the walls. With the dishes done Doris wondered if she could help. "Well, it's for sure that with two of us working we can finish quicker. It would be nice to get this room done. Then while you're at work tomorrow, I can get started on the bedroom. I'll be glad to see the end of this beaver-board and to get all the shavings swept up. The way this place is now, it's an accident waiting to happen. You know, if this thing ever caught fire it would burn like tinder. If we were in bed there would be no chance of getting out alive."

Doris worked at sanding the lower part of the walls, so that she wouldn't have to stand on a chair, but it still made her back ache, and her hands were getting redder by the minute; not hands to work in a dental clinic with. They finally finished, and Jack said he was happy with the job, the walls were now ready for paint, but that could wait for a while. When they were finally in bed, Jack realized he was asking too much of Doris. He raised a subject he had been thinking of for most of the day. He said, "Honey, I know this is one unreasonable hell of a mess I've got us into, but I have been thinking about the mortgage. It has ten years to run. If we have it paid off by then, or even sooner maybe, we will put a mortgage right back on again. The next time we will use the money to build a modern three bedroom bungalow, with an attached two car garage, and instead of having to do all this work ourselves we will hire a contractor." Doris thought that sounded like a "pie in the sky" pipe dream but it sounded good. Then Jack went on to tell her about how he envisioned, the landscaping of a new building site. For one thing, the site should be moved right away from the present location.

He explained that there was a nice level spot right in the northeast corner of their property. All he would need to do was make sure of a water supply, but he told her they could likely find water anywhere, as he thought they had a huge underground lake right below them. Whether or not they'd get water could be established by putting down a test auger.

The more Jack talked, the more enthused he became, which led to his next suggestion. He said, "Do you remember that sign we saw on a farm gate as we drove down from Williston? We thought it such a novel idea, '*El Rancho Costa La Plenty*,' that's what it said. I could make a sign like that for our gate." It took Doris a minute to reply, "Oh, but surely you wouldn't want those words. Just some kind of a slang mixture of Spanish and English that someone thought was cute. We need to think of words that will reflect your Norwegian heritage. We should be able to think of something appropriate. Most of the families we went to school with in Williston could speak Norwegian, you must remember enough of the language yourself. How would this be, 'Welcome to our home. Much love is here.'"

"Sounds okay," said Jack. "Do you know all the Norwegian words to make that up?"

"I think so," said Doris, "just give me a minute. I think I remember them all, except the word for 'our.' Just a minute, I think it is *urser*. Then it would read *Wilkam tu urser hjem. Meget elske ist hia.*"

"I could call Ma to make sure we get it right," said Jack, "her Norwegian is better than her English."

As the conversation went on Doris wished she was an enthused about the future plans for the acreage as she was trying to sound. As for a gate sign, even she liked the idea, because it would be something to take with them, should they eventually give up on trying to make something of the old uncle's holding. She told Jack that there was a sign painter right across the street from the clinic who could likely make a sign just the way they wanted it. Jack thought that would be a waste of money, as he could do it himself as soon as he got time.

Doris had an idea of her own to bring up, but when Jack got so carried away with his dream of a great future for them, she just couldn't bring herself to say it.

When their vows were exchanged she had thought of a cozy little home like her sister had, only without the kids and the diapers, or getting up at night to fix a formula, at least not for a while. No matter what thoughts went through her mind Doris would stick it out, and maybe Jack's dream of a show place would come to pass.

Since arriving at their new home that was not at all what she had pictured, she had been tempted several times to suggest to Jack that they just give it up, go to the bank and tell them they would like to sign a quit claim deed and be out of it. This would mean forfeiting the thousand dollar down payment. Doris wondered if it wouldn't come to that anyway. She would sooner rent something in town, but an apartment would drive Jack mad, and a house would not be much better, so she just couldn't bring up the subject of quitting, not with Jack's enthusiasm.

What else can I say that won't sound too discouraging, thought

Doris, so she said, "But if we built in that corner, wouldn't it put us right across from that cemetery?" Jack replied, "Well, yes, I guess it would, but you know my Aunt Mary is buried there. While we have no way of knowing how the people in the next world see us, I'm sure that if she knew we were living close enough to watch over her, it would make her very happy. She was a wonderful lady, wonder if she still talks with that Irish accent."

The more Jack talked the more enthused he became, as he started telling her how they'd get trees planted right away. "By planting them this summer, we'd have some good sized trees, when we are ready to build. I have seen nice evergreens in some farmyards, and lilacs. Our neighbor in Williston had lilacs, they were beautiful every spring when they bloomed, and smelled nice too." Doris didn't want to dampen his dreams entirely, so she said, "But Jack, landscaping is a trade of its own, and really we wouldn't know much about it. If we just went ahead and planted trees, we'd likely find out later that they were in the wrong place. Before planting anything, it would be best to get some books on landscaping. There are lots of them available, they explain what trees do best, where to put green belts, rock gardens, flower beds, a vegetable garden. Most publications will have a whole array of pictures of look at." Jack couldn't disagree with her. Landscaping was not something to rush into.

The next day, being Friday, was the last day of the work week for Doris, the routine was much the same as the previous day, but Doris knew what the two days off would mean, two days of slavery. She would sooner be at the clinic. If only she could share Jack's feeling about the place. Already he was calling it their plantation. *Aptly named,* thought Doris. *Weren't the plantations in the southern states developed with slave labor?* She wondered if the slaves of that era had worked any harder than she and Jack were doing.

There was a commercial that ran three or four times a day that made Doris think of her own situation. The commercial was promoting some kind of oven cleaner. The scene opened showing a woman on her knees in front of a stove with her head in the oven. Only her butt was visible. Then she backed out of the oven, and was shown wearing a welder's helmet and gloves, as she held an acetylene torch in one hand and a scraper of some kind in the other. She turned to face the camera saying "*This* is marriage." Then a savior came along and sprayed something in the oven and in a few minutes a wipe with a dry cloth had the oven sparkling clean. The words "*This* is marriage," would keep going through her mind as she sandpapered the walls. The words seemed to fit her own situation so well. Marriage as she pictured it did not have this kind of work in it.

The commercial had her wondering if she too could do a commercial, perhaps for some kind of hand lotion, just rub it on her red and blistered hands and the next morning they would be velvety soft and white.

Mistress was becoming very good at controlling the mice. On one occasion when Jack had removed a panel in the bedroom, he saw her with two mice in her mouth, and her paw holding down a third one. He would liked to have got a picture of that, not really to show the cat lady, but it would have made a good conversation piece, if hung on the wall after the renovations were complete. Mistress had spent one night shut in the attic, which she probably hadn't liked much because she howled most of the night, but then the mice probably hadn't liked it much either.

Chapter 6

Tudor, Saskatchewan

With the tragic death of his parents, the funeral, and then settling the estate, Harry had all but forgotten the incident with Lucille Harper. He got a real jolt, by way of a reminder, when Lucille phoned about six weeks later to tell him she was pregnant. Harry's reply might have been expected, "Are you sure?" Then it was "Yes, I am sure." Harry didn't know what to say, so he suggested the idea of an abortion. "Surely you can't mean to murder your own child, can you?" So it came to pass that at nineteen years of age Harry married Lucille Harper. It was only a month after the wedding that Harry found that he had been tricked, Lucille was not pregnant, not even a little bit pregnant.

Even though he had been tricked, he would try and make the marriage work. At any rate they would now have a house of their own. For awhile it seemed everything would go well for Harry and Lucille. Harry got a job at a bank in Moose Jaw, it was now certain that he would not be going to any university. Harry got along well at the bank and within two years was promoted to the position of junior clerk. He was able to commute into Moose Jaw each day for work. It did not cost them much to live as there was no mortgage payment and taxes were minimal. They grew a vegetable garden which reduced the grocery bill.

Harry accepted Lucille's inability to cook as normal for a new bride, as a matter of fact he could think of several jokes about a bride's first efforts in the kitchen that didn't really compliment the new bride on her culinary ability. There was one pun in particular that stood out in his mind. *The couple had been married long enough for the honeymoon to be over, and one day the husband said, "It would be nice if you could make bread like my mother." The wife replies, "And it would be nice if you could make dough like my father."*

Lucille did not get better at anything. As time went on Harry came to realize they had nothing in common and soon realized that the old saying, "Marry in haste, repent at leisure," was more truth than fiction. It was about two years later that he found out about a section in matrimonial law that would allow a marriage to be annulled, but it had to be done in the first six months of the marriage. Well, too late now.

Probably the best way to know a person is to live with them, and the better he came to know Lucille the less he liked about her. Not only was she downright lazy, but her main interest in life was bingo, she was a "bingo nut." She had a friend named Anne who provided transportation for Lucille to all of the bingo parlors. Sometimes they went to Regina, sometimes to Moose Jaw, occasionally to Yorkton, or any other place that happened to put on a bingo game. Lucille was not much of a homemaker. Her addiction to bingo progressed, while her efforts around the house decreased. She seemed to care less and less about the appearance of herself and the house. Any cleaning of the house was done by Harry.

The situation progressed to where Harry was ashamed to invite any of their neighbors in and consequently the time soon came when they were never invited out either. They had no social life.

When Lucille wasn't off to bingo, she was quite happy to sit and watch soap operas and eat junk food. It was a diet she seemed to thrive on, as she gained weight at an alarming pace. It didn't bother her a bit if her jeans were too tight, her sweatshirt too loose to cover the excess fat, or that her clothes were more often than not covered with food stains down the front.

Harry, on the other hand, was very neat in his appearance. Even when he worked in the garden he could be seen wearing clean, pressed clothes, which he, of course, had ironed himself.

Harry was never idle. When he had days off work at the bank, he very often got a job with one of the local farmers. Perhaps driving a grain truck at harvest time, or doing odd jobs repairing or painting buildings. Harry could readily adapt to any task.

He was good friends with Jake Meyer. Jake had a farm on the

outskirts of Tudor, with a good workshop adequately equipped with hand and power tools. It was in this workshop that Harry could often be found. He liked to tinker with stuff, but more than that it was a way to be out of his house and away from Lucille.

Jake had been born to peasant farmers in Germany. His parents owned a small farm some fifty miles east of Berlin. His name was then Jacob Schoen and he was nine years old when the Second World War broke out. Times were very hard during those war years, both of his parents lost their lives during the hostilities. When the Russians moved in on Berlin as the war ended, the Schoen property was confiscated. Jake, now fifteen, was classified as a displaced person. There were many people in war-torn Europe that were in the same situation as Jake. The Allied Nations with their combined strength had brought about the defeat of Germany and it was these nations that set up the Displaced Persons Plan.

Under this plan people like Jake were given a home in one of the allied countries. Any with relatives in one of the hosting countries were usually accepted and given the opportunity to make their new home with these relatives. Jake had had an uncle at Tudor, so it was at the farm of the uncle that Jake had ended up. Jake was still a minor, so the uncle decided it would be in the boy's best interest if he were to legally adopt him. This was how he come to bear the name Meyer, the same as his mother's maiden name.

Jake worked hard for his uncle, who in return treated him well and paid him a just wage for his efforts. As the years went by Jake was able to accumulate a small bank account. By the time he was twenty he was able to rent some land that adjoined his uncle's farm and by using uncle's equipment, Jake did very well. By the time he was twenty-three, a farm with buildings and a complete set-up became available. The owner really wanted to sell it, but as there were no worthwhile offers he agreed to rent it to Jake, with the option to purchase. Eight years later Jake finally became a property owner in the community of Tudor.

Jake moved into the house on the farm that he rented. Now what would be his most needed addition to make his operation a success? Why, a wife of course. Jake had never really done any socializing in his life, there had been no chance in war torn Germany, and since coming to Canada he was just too busy and anyway no one seemed very friendly towards him. He did not realize he was being shunned, he just thought that Canadians were that way. Now to get a wife he must get acquainted, so he started going to church. This was how he had met Helen McGilvary. Helen, while not exactly a raving beauty, was a nice enough girl, and she had just completed high school that June. After a few walks in the park and an afternoon at his farm where they cooked some homemade sausage and drank some lemonade, Jake popped the question and she accepted.

Helen's parents would not even listen to her when she told them how nice she thought Jake was and that she was going to marry him. "What do you mean get married, you have just finished high school. You could go into any kind of a career that you choose, you could have a good future, don't throw your life away on marriage. Wait a few years, travel a bit, find out what the world is about. Get married at your age, no! And to a German at that, why, we just finished a war with those bastards. It's because of them that there are so many Canadians lying in graves all across Europe," they raved. However, the wedding took place anyway without the blessing of her parents. They never even went to the wedding.

Jake and Helen worked hard and they made the farm prosper, but were never accepted as part of the community, not even when they were blessed with children. The kids were considered outcasts too, in school they were referred to as those "German Kids" or that "Kraut Family." Nothing changed for them until the community of Tudor, like most in the province of Saskatchewan, started thinking of their heritage. There should be something put in writing to preserve the area's history, beginning with the first pioneers and up to the present day.

A committee was set up to urge people to reminisce and to collect stories from the residents of Tudor, as well as any of the rural people that got their mail in Tudor. They could write their own story and that of the generation that preceded them, if the first generation were no longer around. Stories of immigration and of settling the area would be welcome. The chairman of the committee was Harry Welks.

It was Harry who encouraged Jake to write the story of his life. Jake was reluctant at first, saying that he was not a pioneer and no one would want his story. Harry did not see the villain in Jake that most did, so he convinced Jake that his story would be welcome. He said, "Look, Jake, there has been tons of stuff written by people of the Allied Nations regarding the rise and fall of Nazi Germany, maybe it's time someone told of the ways things were, as seen through the eyes of Germany's working people. Tell us what you were led to believe. Even though you were not very old, you must remember some of it. Then lead your tale up to how you came to be in Tudor. That's what the Tudor history will be about, how people came to be here. If you have a problem with phrasing, I am sure Helen could help you, as long as you tell the story."

So a very touching story came from the Meyer family. Many of the community were moved by it, and from then on, slowly but surely, the neighbors finally decided that maybe that German fella wasn't so bad after all. Really it wasn't his fault that Canadians were lying in graves across Europe. Jake didn't care that much for himself, but he was glad that the children would have things a bit better than he'd had.

Chapter 7

Bismark, North Dakota

With the renovation project somewhat under control, Jack decided he should be bringing home a paycheque too, he looked around at some of the garages, but the new vehicles were so computerized, he knew he would need a mechanic's course to obtain work in that field. He discarded the idea of working as a mechanic. Since he knew a good deal about tires, he tried the Goodyear Tire franchise. They hired him to work in the shop, he started on Thursday morning. His hours were eight to five, the same as Doris worked, they were able to ride together to work.

The following Monday morning they left early and took Mistress back to the cat lady. It was a couple of days later than they were supposed to bring her back, but Jack explained his way out of trouble, by telling her that they were enjoying Mistress and her family so much they just lost track of time. Doris almost had to laugh as he told her how well the kittens had settled in, and they even seemed to like the VCR tape but they couldn't sit still as long as Mistress. *You liar*, thought Doris, *you never even hooked up the VCR, much less let the kittens in the house.* The lady told Jack she was glad the kittens had a good home, but that she would take Mistress to a vet and have her spayed, so there would be no more kittens. *A splendid idea*, thought Doris, and told Jack as they drove away that they should do that with one of the kittens, that orange one, if it was a female. "Then, if we got her sandbox trained she could become our house pet." That is exactly what did happen, they called her Ginger. Ginger became a member of the household till she finally died of old age.

After two weeks on the job the manager asked Jack if he would like to work on the road. The company supplied him with a service truck, a two-way radio, and a pager. The dispatcher contacted Jack when a call came in and Jack headed to the specified location to do the repair. Jack was on twenty-four hour call five days a week. This suited Jack just fine as the pay would be good and he would still have time to work on the house renovations. This would work well as it left their own truck free for Doris to use as needed. Jack and Doris were finally starting to feel more confident about themselves.

After they returned Mistress to the cat lady, the Nelsons realized that while the mice were no longer the problem that had faced them to start with, they were still not eradicated entirely. Jack told Doris, they'd have to have mouse traps in both the cellar and the attic, or the things would multiply and the problem would be right back with them. The kittens were not mousers yet. On a couple of occasions Jack had managed to kill a mouse with a good swat with a broom, then thrown the dead mouse to the kittens. They would play with it, but the instinct to hunt had not developed yet.

Doris didn't like the idea of a trap, "Oh, but the poor things would have to suffer so much if they were caught by a leg and held all night. They would be so frightened." Jack assured her that there was a trap on the market that was quite humane, the mouse was contained but in no way injured. He went on to explain what it was like, "It's a metal box, with two compartments. One half has a hole through from one side to the other. The natural curiosity of the mouse causes it to run through the hole. As it does it's own weight releases a spring, and the platform it is on rotates a complete turn, and in doing so the mouse gets dropped into the second compartment. The mouse is in no way hurt, but it can't escape because the box it is in has metal sides that mouse can't dig his claws into, so it can't do any climbing."

It was with some reluctance that Doris agreed to try and keep the population controlled with the trap method. It went well until the next morning when Jack checked the trap in the attic, and found it had two live mice in it. To dispose of them, Jack immersed them in a bucket of water, trap and all, until they were completely dead by drowning. Doris thought this so cruel, "Couldn't you just let them go?"

Jack said, "But, honey, they would just come right back in the house again."

"Well, if you took them away, maybe a mile or so, surely they wouldn't get back." Jack agreed to this. With two more caught the next morning he took them a mile up the road, but before opening the lid on the box he gave it a real good shaking. When he opened the lid and let the mice fall on the hard road, they were too stunned to move for a while, thus allowing Jack to step on them before they could get away. He never told Doris about the final end of the operation. What she didn't know wouldn't hurt her.

The war news was also sounding better. President Nixon had made several announcements about something called "peace with honor." He also told the American people that the brave and worthy service-men and women would be back on American soil very soon. Twenty thousand troops were to be withdrawn in June and another group was to be withdrawn in December. Jack liked what he was hearing. The war was over, he had avoided the draft, and the future looked bright.

It was getting into the latter part of March, the grass was greening up a bit, so they thought it would be good if they could buy a milk cow. This would give them a wholesome product for the table and also make use of the grass. They didn't have a lot of money left after spending so much on the house, but they would go to the next Saturday's livestock auction mart to see what a cow might cost.

One thing they found out was that they didn't have enough money to buy a cow. "Do you think your dad would lend us the money?" said Jack. Doris agreed to phone and ask him. They called that evening. Of course he wanted to know how much they needed and what they planned to buy. Yes, he would let them have $300.00 at 3 percent interest. They could sign a promissory note that would set the repayments at twenty dollars a month.

"Did they think they could handle that?" They got the money but Jack had some uncomplimentary thoughts about his father-in-law.

"Damn him," said Jack. "I'd sooner deal with the cat lady." But Doris explained to him it was just her dad's way, he was teaching them how the business world operates. Nothing was ever done on a handshake, and 3 percent was a heck of a lot below the current rate of bank interest.

Chapter 8

The Auction Ring

With the cheque from Doris' father deposited in their bank account, the young couple went to the auction mart the following Saturday. This time they fully intended to buy a cow and get their start in the livestock business. The mart was located on the outskirts of Bismark and about three miles north of the cemetery corner. There were a lot of corrals, platforms, unloading ramps, and the like, all painted white.

Other than for their brief foray to the place last week, when they had found out that to buy a cow as intended would take money, they didn't know anything about an auction ring. A good sized crowd was already there, but they saw seats for two people in the fourth row. Each row of seats was at a higher level than the row in front of it, thus everyone had a good view of the auction ring. They were impressed with the ring, it had a concrete floor that had a generous covering of clean sawdust on it. It was an oval-shaped structure enclosed by a cement wall about waist high, steel posts were set about four feet apart in the cement. Three strands of steel cable evenly spaced were threaded through holes in the posts, thus bringing the total height of the enclosure to about six feet, and still not obstructing the view of the spectators. A metal gate at each end completed the enclosure except for two steel posts set in the cement floor, at each end of the ring and just beside the gates. The Nelsons didn't know the purpose of the posts, noting they were only a little over a foot from the wall and about eight inches apart. They would learn later in the day as to the need for the posts. That completed the ring except for the auctioneer's dais, an enclosed platform about four feet high and situated against the solid rear wall of the building.

The auctioneer opened the sale with welcoming remarks to the crowd, and then introduced the two men on the floor of the ring.

They were his ring men and could take bids as well as he could. Then it was down to business. The entry gate opened and about six calves, less than a week old, came into the ring. The auctioneer said, "You will be bidding for choice, the highest bidder can pick the calf of their choice, or take as many as they wish, at that many times the money."

From then on the Nelsons couldn't understand anything he said, to Doris the words sounded like, "dyonng bnong mnong slonng." The ring men were active as they waved, and beckoned to prospective buyers, every little while one of them would clap his hands, make a military about-turn, point his arm to the auctioneer like a marksman with a pistol on a firing range, and holler "Yohhhe." When his mate did it, the call would be "Gohhhe." Doris soon had them identified as Mr. Yo and Mr. Go.

A couple more entries that didn't interest Jack and Doris, then an all black cow that had a black calf with a white face came through the gate. Doris thought the calf was so cute, she whispered to Jack, saying, "Wouldn't it be nice if we could buy them." Jack whispered back that it would likely take more money than they had. The auctioneer said, "We'll sell the baldy first." Nelsons didn't know what he meant, but a black baldy is the offspring of an Aberdeen Angus cow that has been cross-bred to a herd-sire of the Hereford breed. The result of the cross produces the black calf with a white face.

The auctioneer went into a chant that they couldn't understand, but once they were sure he said, "Going for a mere one hundred twenty-five dollars." The Nelsons again started whispering to each other, "Gee, that seems cheap enough, maybe there is something wrong with them." The auctioneer had said "Wave your catalogue to bid," the next bid would be one hundred fifty dollars. Surely they couldn't go wrong at that, so Jack waved his catalogue. The auctioneer said, "Ah, ha, we have a new bidder in the crowd, the bid is one and one half and who'll make it one hundred seventy-five" and then some more chanting.

There was a gentleman of about sixty years, sitting beside the Nelsons, he was wearing a western hat, a leather coat, and blue jeans. He had been noticing Jack and Doris ever since they took their seat beside him. He had already decided the kids were new to the ring and weren't too sure of what they were doing, as they got such strange looks on their faces as they muttered and whispered to each other. As a matter of fact he felt sorry for them, so when they got the bid at one hundred fifty dollars he said, "I hope you realize that it's only the calf you're bidding on and not both of them." Oh! They hadn't known that, "Can we tell one of those men that we didn't know it was only the calf and withdraw our bid?" The man in the felt hat said, "Well, don't worry about it for a minute and we'll see what happens, just sit on your catalogue, so you can't wave it again."

The auctioneer kept on with his chant, and on occasion saying something they could understand. He was still trying to get one hundred seventy-five, but without any response. He was holding a wooden mallet in the air, and ready to hit the desk top in front of him, as he would say "Sold." Just before that happened, Felt Hat, as Doris began to think of him, yelled out, "Would you take a five dollar bill?" Five plus the one hundred fifty bid by the Nelsons would bring the selling price to one hundred fifty-five dollars. The auctioneer said, "Well, I guess it's still money." So after a bit more chanting and asking for a bid of one hundred sixty that never came, the mallet came down as the auctioneer said, "Sold to the gentleman in the fourth row for one hundred fifty-five dollars." Jack and Doris were out of their predicament, and Felt Hat owned a calf that he probably didn't want.

The next animal to enter the ring was a two year old heifer. Her first action was to put her head down and make a run straight at Mr. Go. Before she could attack him, Mr. Go stepped behind the two posts at his end of the ring. As Mr. Yo stepped behind the ones at his end, the Nelsons could see the need for the posts that until now had not seemed to have any purpose. With no open targets in the ring to vent her anger on, the heifer decided to leave the ring. That waist-high wall between her and the people seated in the stands must have looked like an easy bolt to freedom. Maybe she didn't see the steel cables above the cement wall, because she leapt right into them. The cables not only prevented her escape, but when stretched to their limit acted like a catapult, as she fell into the ring on her back. Her jump at the cables had the effect of clearing the first few rows in the stands of people. Can't blame them for their reaction, when they saw about a thousand pounds of beef hurtling towards them. It was a wonder they didn't injure each other in their scramble.

The animal was again on her feet, and making useless passes at the ring men, still safe behind their respective posts. The auctioneer said to the man behind the exit gate, "Open up and let her out of here before she hurts herself." To the stands he said, "There's nothing wrong with her, folks, she's just nervous in a crowd. I had a girl-friend like that once, if I took her to a dance I would have to sit out in the car with her." Some of the people laughed.

Felt Hat said to the Nelsons, "He's used that joke before, it's time he thought of a new one."

The Nelsons could see an alleyway between the holding pens as the gate opened, letting the enraged animal trot off out of sight. The bidding and chanting went on, with the ring empty. Doris said to Felt Hat, "What is he selling? There's nothing in the ring?"

Felt Hat replied, "He's still selling the one that just left the ring. It's okay, buyers have seen her and know what they are bidding on."

Felt Hat asked them what sort of livestock they were interested in. They told him about their recently acquired acreage and their idea of getting a milk cow. "Good thinking," said Felt Hat, "I'm sure some-thing will come along that's going to be just what you want. How about this one," he said, as a blue roan cow entered the ring.

The auctioneer said, "Now, here's the one you've all been waiting for, she's just three years old and will be having her second calf in about two weeks time. And listen to this," he continued, "she is a granddaughter of Kitty Clay, that high producer raised by the Clay Brothers over in Wisconsin. They put her on the show circuit, and for three years in a row Kitty Clay stood first in the Denver open. And if that isn't enough," said the auctioneer, "she is carrying the service of a grandson of Diamond Dundee, that great herd-sire imported right from Scotland by that well known breeder in Minnesota, Simon Macleod."

"Yes, folks a real valuable package, all nicely put together for you. Who'd like to open the bidding at a thousand dollars."

Doris said to Felt Hat, "Is she really going to bring that much?"

Felt Hat said, "No, and he knows it. Just a trick of his to make you think you're in on a bargain, when the bidding starts a bit lower."

Doris said, "All that he said about her pedigree, is that right?"

"Probably," said Felt Hat, "but it doesn't mean much when you think about it. Sure she's a granddaughter of Kitty Clay, that gives her one quarter of grandma's bloodline, but what about the other three-quarters? Might be something you wouldn't want at all. And it's the same with the calf she's going to have, it will have one eighth of the bloodline of old Diamond Dundee. Just ignore that little speech he gave, he does it all the time. It's part of the business of auctioning, and he's good at it. Has to be, because that's how he makes his living.

"Pay no attention to what you heard, and look at the animal in front of you. I think she shows a lot of promise. Her body is well proportioned. She's young, so there's a lot of years ahead of her. Her udder looks sound, her teats are long enough to grasp properly to milk her. She has a wide forehead, with eyes spaced well apart, indicating an animal that will have a gentle disposition. You should stay away from the ones with a long narrow face, and eyes so close together that they're almost coming out of the same socket. Animals like that are hard keepers with a mean disposition.

Doris said, "Oh," while thinking, *There is a lot more to the cattle industry than we realized, and we were lucky to have taken a seat beside a knowledgeable person like Felt Hat.*

Felt Hat went on to say, "Yes, I think she is likely just what you are looking for."

The auctioneer was still asking for the thousand, but changed and said, "Well, who wants to start her at five hundred?"

Felt Hat said, "No, he won't get that either." He then went on to warn the kids about the auctioneer taking bids from the Rafter Brothers. "The Rafter Brothers," said Doris, "who are they?"

"They don't exist," said Felt Hat, "but if he's got a buyer on that he is pretty sure is going to bid again, he will manufacture the next increment in the bidding sequence right out of thin air, so to obtain the item they want the prospects bid again. It's called a bid from the Rafter Brothers because to get his imaginary bid, the bidder is always sitting in the top row right near the roof of the building. Once in a while he will get caught at it, but will squirm out of it by saying to somebody in the top row, 'Well, weren't you in the blue shirt bidding? No, well I'm sorry, now where were we.'"

Felt Hat went on to say, "It's a strange thing but that manufactured bid not only comes from someone in the top row, but he's always wearing a blue shirt." Felt Hat then offered a suggestion by saying, "Would you like me to bid for you, he won't try any funny stuff with me, I've been around too long."

"Oh, yes," said Jack and Doris in unison.

The auctioneer said, "Well, start her where you like then. It's where we finish that counts, not where we start." Felt Hat held up three fingers. The auctioneer said, "Thank you, I'm bid three hundred dollars in the fourth row. Who wants to make it four?" No response. The auctioneer said, "Four and four and four, dnonng, lnonng, mnonng and four and four, do I hear four hundred dollars?" A movement in the front row by a man in a red windbreaker caught Doris' eye, he held his hand in front of him flat with the palm down, and waved it back and forth. Neither of the Nelsons knew what his signal meant. In the sign language of the auction ring, the signal meant the bidder was offering half of the increment increase the auctioneer is asking for.

"I've got a bid of three hundred fifty in the front row, and thank you sir," said the auctioneer," I'd never of thought of doing that."

Felt Hat said, "B.S. There's more excrement coming out of that guy's mouth than there is out of the cattle going through the ring." "And now you in the fourth row. Make an even four?"

Felt Hat made the same kind of a motion with his hand that Windbreaker in the front row had done, saying to no one in particular, "If he can take a half bid in the front row, he can take one from me."

The auctioneer said, "I've got a bid of three hundred seventy-five, and now, sir, in the front row, will you make it an even four?" Windbreaker in the front row rolled his hand over, with his thumb pointing up. Mr. Yo pointed to the auctioneer and yelled, "Yohhhe."

"And now close it out with four hundred twenty-five in the fourth row?" said the auctioneer.

Felt Hat turned to the Nelsons to ask them how high they planned to go. The auctioneer said, "There is a family conference going on in the fourth row, we'll give them a bit of time."

Jack said, "We really don't have enough money to go any more than four hundred."

Felt Hat said, "That's a neighbor of mine in the front row that's bidding against you. He doesn't want her, he's got lots of cattle already, he just thinks she's a good investment. If you felt you could handle it, another bid of ten bucks will likely get her." After a bit of whispering to each other, Jack said, "It would stretch our budget a bit but okay, but no more than ten more dollars."

Felt Hat put up both hands with all ten fingers outstretched. Auctioneer said, "I got a bid of four hundred ten dollars, you in the front row make it four hundred twenty-five." Windbreaker did nothing. A bit more chanting by the auctioneer and he finally brought the mallet down and said, "Sold in the fourth row for four hundred ten dollars. Sam, are you bidding for yourself or those people beside you?" Felt Hat pointed to the Nelsons. Doris was glad to know that Felt Hat had a name.

The auctioneer said, "Is this your first venture into the cattle industry?" They both nodded. The auctioneer said, "Well, congratulations, you've bought a good one for a start, but don't go away. There's more coming in that I'm sure you will like." Jack and Doris both smiled.

Before they could do anything else a runner was up in the stands with a piece of paper they would have to sign, acknowledging their purchase. Doris read it and Jack signed it. There was an item on it that Doris didn't understand, eighty cents for insurance, so she asked Felt Hat, now known as Sam, what that was for.

Sam said, "Don't let that bother you, because it's good protection, not likely to help you if you're taking your cow out right away, but there are some that don't get their purchase till the next day. The insurance covers the animal from the time of purchase until you take it out of here. If while still on the premises an animal is injured or dies, the insurance company will reimburse your full purchase price. It's rare but it's been known to happen." They thanked Sam for his help, and then went to the cashier's cage, located just beside the door from outside. Upon receipt of their cheque, the cashier gave them a gate pass, telling them to present it to one of the yard men out back.

The yard man asked if they were loading into a truck or a low bellied trailer. "Neither," said Jack. "We don't have far to go, so I plan to lead her." The yard man said, "Well, have you a halter, or something." Jack went to the half ton, and got the rope that he had bought when he needed something to tie down those insulation batts, saying to Doris, "I knew I would need this sometime for something." The yard man took the rope from Jack and as it was quite long folded it double. Then with a few twists and knots, he soon fashioned a headstall that fit the cow perfectly, and still had a loose end of about five feet, for a lead rope. Doris couldn't believe how fast he did that. He called it a hackamore.

Then it was out of the pens and onto the road. Jack soon realized it would be easier on the cow's feet if he led her in the ditch. It took a bit of a tug on the lead rope once in awhile, as the new possession tried to get a mouthful of grass when she could. Doris followed with the truck, but found it all but impossible to drive that slowly. The only way was just to stop, let Jack get a little ahead, then move the truck on till she caught up again. After about a half a mile with no real problem, Doris wondered if she might just as well go on home. Jack told her, "Yes, by all means, I'll be okay."

Doris said, "I'll have a pitcher of cold lemonade ready for you."

Jack said, "That sounds good, I should be there in less than an hour."

When he got home Doris not only had the lemonade ready, but she said, "I've picked out a name for our cow. How does Bluebell sound to you?"

Jack replied, "She should like that, a very fitting name for a blue cow."

Chapter 9

Tudor, Saskatchewan

Nine years had passed since Harry and Lucille were married, and heaven knows he had tried to make it work. It was coming to a point where Harry knew the only way to make his loveless marriage with Lucille bearable was to keep busy elsewhere. The Tudor history with its stories of pioneer life had aroused the interest of both Harry and Jake in antiques. As a result they had become involved in restoring old cars whenever they had any spare time, currently they were working on a 1928 Chandler.

Harry had given up trying to get Lucille to do something about her appearance, or to look after the home the way most wives did. Thank God their union had not produced any children. Harry admittedly was glad when Lucille was away at one of her bingo games, leaving him home alone.

Harry had some help thinking about what the future might hold. Irma Soelen was a waitress in the café next door to the bank. Irma was not only good looking, but also had a quick wit and a charming personality. Irma had at one time thought of trying to get into the theatrical world by becoming a ballet dancer. She was good enough at it but gave up the idea because of the cost, and anyway there was no guarantee of any future in it. She was accepted as a member of the "dream team" for the Saskatchewan Roughrider Football Club. These were a group of young girls that provided entertainment for the fans at half time, as well as the times the game was stopped for the running of a television commercial. The people at home watching TV had to look at the commercial, while the fans at the game were able to enjoy the antics of the girls as they did their dance routines and drills, waving their pom-poms. Irma stayed with the dream team for two years. It didn't pay much, but she got to see a lot of Canada for free as the football team traveled from one city to another and, as she said, it was fun.

Irma, like Harry, was trapped in a loveless match. Harry, like every one else, wondered why she had married an oaf like Bud Soelen. The general consensus was that she had felt sorry for him, and probably thought she could make him over. Harry had known Bud for a long time. Bud could never do anything right. As a kid, he was overgrown and really clumsy at any kind of sport. A phrase from a story in one of Aesop's Fables, *The Ugly Duckling*, might be applied to Bud, "maybe he stayed in the egg too long." At age fourteen, he was well over six feet tall and weighed close to two hundred pounds. The saying that "he had two left feet" fitted him well. He was a real failure in class. He eventually dropped out of school at age sixteen, after reaching only about Grade five or six level. Presently he was employed by the city as a helper on a garbage truck. He liked to call himself a sanitary engineer.

Harry had been going to the café next door for his lunch even before Irma came to work there. The last few months, the calls to the café had also included morning coffee breaks.

Irma and Harry's relationship was growing closer as time went on. Two weeks ago, they had managed to slip away to the horse races in Regina. Lucille had been on one of her bingo jaunts and Bud was on a "bender" with his drinking pals.

It was Friday morning in mid-October during a morning coffee break that Irma told Harry she had the afternoon off. She suggested it would be nice to go for a drive in the country, before all the autumn leaves were gone. Harry said he would check with his manager to see if he could get the afternoon off.

When asked, Harry's manager said, "Okay," as mid-month was not a busy time anyway. At noon Harry took his car from the parking lot behind the bank and drove it out onto the street, parking in front of the café. It took Irma less than two minutes to get out of the café and into the front seat of Harry's car.

Through the plate glass window of the hardware store across the street, Bud Soelen watched Harry drive away with Irma at his side. Bud immediately got into his own car which was parked out front.

He had to wait for a traffic light to change at Main Street, he then turned left toward the Trans-Canada Highway. It wasn't long before Bud spotted Harry's car about two blocks ahead, also going in the direction of the highway. When Harry turned onto the eastbound lane, Bud followed at a discreet distance.

Harry and Irma turned off the highway a short distance east of Moose Jaw and drove up to the office of a small motel, Bud kept on going. He would let them have their fun, but he had other ideas for Harry. Bud had never liked Harry, he was always a show-off, and made everyone believe he was superior.

Bud drove back into Moose Jaw and went to a car rental agency. He rented a car, the same make and color as Harry's car. He then drove out to Tudor and parked in the Welk's driveway.

When Lucille opened the door to see Bud standing there, she didn't have much choice but to have him come in, even though she had never liked Bud very much.

Bud immediately got to the point of filling her in on their spouse's activities. "If you don't believe me," said Bud, "phone the motel and find out for yourself." Lucille said, "No, I don't really care what they do as long as I have a roof over my head and credit at the local store." Bud wanted to be a bit more convincing, so he looked up the phone number and dialed the motel himself. When the motel answered, he asked if they had a Harry Welks registered there. No, they had no one by that name, they only had one room rented at the moment, and that was to a Graham Brown.

"Well would you be good enough to ring Mr. Brown's room for me please?" Bud intoned sweetly. He could hear the phone ringing, but before anyone could answer, Bud handed the phone to Lucille, saying, "Here, you can talk to them." Lucille still didn't want to talk, so when Irma answered, she just asked if Philip was there? Irma said, "No, you must have the wrong number, there is no Philip here."

Bud wanted to know what she did that for, and who had answered. Lucille told him, it could have been Irma, but it really didn't matter to her. Lucille was waiting for Anne who was going to pick her up in half an hour, as they were going to Yorkton to play bingo. There was a mini-bingo tonight and the "big one" was the next day. There was going to be a one hundred thousand dollar payout, so who could worry about anything else! Lucille told Bud to leave and said, "Talk to Irma and Harry yourself if you are so worried."

Lucille then went to the bathroom. Instead of leaving, Bud went into the storeroom off the kitchen. In the deep freeze he found a frozen fish that probably weighed about eight pounds. The fish was wrapped in cellophane with head and tail intact.

When Lucille came out of the bathroom, Bud was behind her with the fish grasped firmly by the tail. One quick blow to the back of the head dropped Lucille to the hallway floor. She was quickly rolled to her back and a few good cracks across the temple succeeded in crushing her skull. Bud returned the fish to the deep freeze, thinking what a stupid bitch Lucille was.

He then went into the bedroom and opened a few dresser drawers, spilling some of the contents on the floor. Just a half-hearted attempt to make it appear that robbery was the motive for the crime.

Then it was into the rental car and back to the agency in Moose Jaw. The car had only been gone about an hour, so other than a piece of paper in the files, hardly anyone at the agency knew it had been gone.

Bud then went to the bar and spent the rest of the day and evening getting absolutely stone drunk. Most of the patrons didn't know when Bud came in, but thought he had likely been there since the bar opened at eleven o'clock. When he returned home around midnight, Irma sure thought he smelled like he had been in a bar all day.

After the phone call to the motel room, Irma told Harry she thought it was Lucille who had called. They wondered what she was up to and who put her up to it.

They had already agreed to start some kind of a procedure that would free them from their hopeless marriages. They also thought it would be better if no one knew of their involvement with each other.

Harry took Irma back to Moose Jaw, and let her out a few blocks from home. He then left Moose Jaw for the village of Tudor, but did not go home. He went to the farm of his friend, Jake Meyer, on the outskirts of Tudor.

After working on the restoration of the Chandler for a while, and after Harry had painted the spokes in a couple of wheels, Harry asked Jake if he could do him a favor.

"Sure, anything friend," Jake replied. So Harry explained his involvement with Irma, and his plans to get out of his marriage to Lucille. He also told Jake about the phone call to the motel room.

"So in case anyone ever asks, I would like you to say I have been here since about twelve-thirty P.M. today. It would take me about that long to get here from the bank, after getting off work at noon."

"No problem, old buddy," said Jake as he thought to himself, he sure didn't blame Harry for having a roving eye, considering that "tub of lard" he was married to. Jake had always thought the Michelin Tire Company could have used her in their commercial instead of that stack of tires they had wired together to resemble a human form.

Chapter 10

Bismark, North Dakota

Bluebell didn't take two weeks before giving birth to a bull calf. Just a week after they bought her, a calf they would call Argus came into the world. Neither Jack nor Doris knew anything about cattle, but to get milk you must have to squeeze those teats in the appropriate manner to get milk to squirt into a pail. That part of it was all right, but the stuff they got! It sure didn't look like any milk they had ever seen. It was thick and yellow, with about the consistency of yellow paint. Was there something wrong with Bluebell? Was the milk safe for Argus to drink? Was this actually what unprocessed milk looked like?

Jack said, "Let's call Ma, she was born on a farm in Norway and lived there until she was fourteen, you know, then the whole family emigrated to the United States. I'll bet she knows something about cattle."

Sophia was happy to hear from them. It was a relief to hear her say, "It is normal for the first milkings to be high in colostrum content, this gets the calf's digestive system working. As I recollect, it is important for the calf to have a bowel movement within the first twenty-four hours. If it doesn't I would call the veterinarian if I were you." She went on to tell the story of her father's efforts to get calves to nurse, and what seemed to work was pushing the calf against the cow's flank and holding a teat right in its mouth to get him started, after a couple of feedings the calves seemed to get the idea. After the calf got enough to be satisfied, it would be all right to milk out any left in the udder for themselves. She added a warning, about not using the milk for themselves, until the colostrum dropped to a normal level. This would take about four or five days.

Once the milk was okay to use, she told them it would be best to take the calf right away from the cow and teach it to drink from a pail. "Argus won't like it at first but when he is hungry enough, he will drink. You can get him started by holding your fingers in its mouth and when it starts sucking your finger, push his nose into a pail with the milk in it."

Jack placed his hand over the mouthpiece of the phone and said, "Doris, I think we have created a monster, she won't shut up about the damn cow." Mrs. Nelson went on to suggest they get a cream separator, so they could separate the cream from the milk. The skim milk would be all right for the calf, if a supplement was added. "Lots of supplements on the market and by the time the calf is three months old it will start to nibble on a few oats and grass," she carried on. "You know, Jack, with the cream Doris could make butter, or with the berry season coming lots of people will pay a good price to buy a pint of cream. There is just nothing like a bowl of fresh raspberries with real cow's cream."

Another thing she told them was then they took the calf away from its mother they would both make quite a fuss. Just like any mother losing a baby. They were told not to get soft-hearted when they started to bawl. In about three days both mother and calf would be over it, especially if they were separated so they couldn't see each other.

The phone call finally came to an end with Sophia wishing them luck with their new farming experiences.

After a few tumbles, some skinned shins, and many good laughs Bluebell and Argus settled into their routine.

With plans for a garden, along with the milk Bluebell would give them, plus some of her offspring to market when ready, the future did indeed look promising. They had tried to visit Uncle Andrew once since coming to the acreage, but he must have been heavily sedated, because they weren't able to get any response from him when they told him who they were. If they could forget the problem they had had with the mice, the rest of the deal with Andrew looked good, and they thought it could be as he said, they could produce half their living right on the acreage. With the two paycheques coming in, they were planning a budget. As soon as they had some garden produce, a drop in the grocery bill would follow. Doris was the one doing the arithmetic, balancing their income against the amount they would need to spend. She told Jack that her cheque would be enough to live on, Jack's cheque would go into a separate account that would be drawn from for capital expenses only. It would be used for the mortgage payments, and for taxes. With careful planning the mortgage could be paid off in about three years, or four at the most.

Once the current mortgage was out of the way, they would take out another one that would let them start to build their dream home, with its two-car garage. As the visions danced through their minds on a daily basis, they could already see the trees as they grew taller, while the flowers blossomed with the most radiant of colors.

Perhaps they could buy another cow next year, the money would of course come out of the capital account, and have double the income for the sale of fresh cream. Not only would another animal be company for Bluebell, but once the offspring reached market age there would be twice the income from that source too. Just as Andrew had said, there was plenty of grass. The picture was shaping up nicely.

The next day a card came in the mail from the post office, advising Jack he had some registered mail to be picked up.

They had all but forgotten about it, but there it was, Jack's draft notice. This time there would be no exemption. He was to report on May 2, 1972, to Fort Bragg in North Carolina for military training. Why so far away? Well, who knows how the army thinks?

With tearful goodbyes Jack and Doris parted, inwardly hoping that the news from Vietnam was real and the war would soon be over. Maybe after a short stint in boot camp, he would be home again. To add good news to bad, Doris thought she was pregnant.

Jack Nelson adjusted to military life readily enough. He was in good physical shape, so the route marches, early rising, and drills were no problem. Some of the officers were obnoxious, but Jack had taken orders most of his life, so he could live with them. He just lived to get the stint over with and be back with Doris.

Then came the notice, they were being sent to Vietnam. The entire camp, one thousand troops. It was unbelievable. President Nixon said troops were being withdrawn, the American military was supposed to be coming home. So much for the Commander in Chief! They would be leaving on a troop carrier from New York, August 1. Just ninety days after Jack had arrived at camp.

The troops were all given a week's leave before they were to report in New York. Jack and Doris were glad of their few days together, though Doris was disappointed to see him use so much of the time doing still more work on the old house. She told him he should just leave it until he returned home again. He responded by telling her if he could get the baseboard on and the trim around the windows, it would be one less thing to think about doing. He had saved enough of his army pay to buy the molding to finish the trim in all three rooms. He told Doris that with that much out of the way she might want to look for some different curtains. That part of it was all fine, but she just wished that for once he could think of something besides work.

The week's leave went by all too quickly and it was a sad goodbye when the time came for Jack to go to the airport and be on his way to somewhere called Vietnam. By then Doris had confirmed that she was pregnant and could only hope Jack would be home again before he became a father.

As a going-away present Doris gave Jack a locket, with a miniature picture of herself in it. Jack promised to wear it next to his heart.

Chapter 11

Tudor, Saskatchewan

Lucille's friend Anne lived with her mother in the same block as the Welks, but across the back lane, and three houses to the left. Anne, now over twenty-five years old, had never married, and with her looks it was understandable. She did not have a steady job, but worked part-time at a local restaurant, and sometimes did some babysitting. The one thing she had going for her was her ability to grow a garden. Some said she had a green thumb, as she had won so many prizes for various produce entries at the local fairs. She managed to have quite a bit of in-season produce for sale, which helped to supplement the household income.

At about three o'clock on that fatal afternoon, she had backed her car out of the garage and into the lane. Then the short drive took her to the rear of the Welks' residence, where she stopped. Leaving the motor running, she went to the Welks' back door. She entered without knocking, as she always did, expecting Lucille to be ready for the trip to Yorkton.

The grisly scene that she was greeted with sent her into hysterics. Instead of phoning the police, she went screaming back to her mother's house, leaving the car where it was with the motor still running. Between screams and sobs her mother finally got the story of what had happened. It was her mother who took charge and phoned the police.

The police responded within fifteen to twenty minutes. An ambulance arrived a short time later. The police followed the standard procedure for any homicide case. They took pictures, dusted for fingerprints, checked for signs of forced entry and searched for the murder weapon. The deep freeze readily caught their eye because Bud had left a plastic bag hanging out of the deep freeze's lid.

The frozen fish was lying in a wire basket at the top of the freezer, blood and hair adhering to the cello-wrap. The police inspector took a close-up photo before touching any part of it. He then lifted the fish and cut away a portion of the cello-wrap containing the most blood. He returned the fish to the freezer and placed the cello sample in a container marking it, "Exhibit A." The body was then transported by ambulance to the crime lab.

Anne's mother made her drink some hot chamomile tea in an effort to calm her down. As she was still quite distraught, the police questioning was brief. There was no way she would go back into the Welks' home. About all they got out of her was the approximate time of entry, and no, she had not touched anything in the house. She also told them of their plans to go to Yorkton. They ended the interview by telling her to move her car out of the back lane. It was Anne's mother who brought the car home, and parked it in their garage.

Harry left the Meyer farm at approximately four-thirty. It was about fifteen to twenty minutes after Harry left that Helen came out to the shop with the news she had heard from a neighbor. There had been a murder in town. As she explained who it was and gave details, the wheels in Jake's head began to turn.

Jake gave the matter some thought and decided that providing an alibi for a bit of hanky-panky was one thing, but murder! He couldn't really believe Harry would resort to murder to get out of that loveless marriage he had been tricked into. *Oh yes, Jack knew the full story in connection with Lucille's scheming.* But the more he pondered the more he thought, *Why else would he need an alibi for his whereabouts for the afternoon?* Jake remembered the term C.Y.A.: cover your ass. So for his own protection he phoned Crime Stoppers.

When Harry returned home, he drove down the back lane and parked in the vacant lot across the back alley from his house. He entered the kitchen through the back door. Had he driven down the street, he would have noticed that his house was cordoned off with yellow tape. If he had gone in the front room he would have noticed the answering machine was flashing, indicating a waiting message. If he had gone to the bedroom, he would have noticed the dresser drawers in a mess. Lucille had told him she was leaving for Yorkton that afternoon, so he would not have worried about it. He would have thought she had been looking for one of her good-luck charms to take to bingo. If Harry had parked in his driveway, the police would have noticed he was home and would have called.

But Harry never went any further than the kitchen and adjoining storeroom. Had he been a bit more observant he would have noticed the bloodstain on the hall carpet. But he could be excused for missing it, since not only was the carpet a rust colour that allowed the bloodstain to blend well, but it was many years old, so had lots of worn and stained spots. Harry often thought about replacing all the carpeting, but with Lucille's lack of interest in housekeeping, he had just thought, *What's the use.*

Lucille had not left anything out for supper, but then she never did. Harry thought about the salmon he had bought off the fish truck from British Columbia. He could bake that and make a few slices of toast. The fish would be too much for one meal, but he could make a salmon loaf for tomorrow. Lucille would not be home until Sunday. Maybe he would give Irma a call, to see if she would care to come out and share the salmon loaf with him. They had agreed not to be seen together, but as the days were getting shorter now, almost dark by six, she could park across the back lane and no one would notice.

With this happy thought in mind and a smile on his lips, Harry went about preparing the salmon. He stripped away the cello wrap, throwing it in the garbage. *I don't remember this wrapping being so messy when I bought the fish,* Harry unconsciously thought. While the fish was thawing, Harry did up the dishes that were still in the sink from breakfast. He was not surprised that Lucille had not bothered with them. The salmon now thawed, Harry removed the head and tail, quickly scraped away the scales, and finished getting it ready for the oven.

Once he had it in the baking pan, he placed a few stripes of bacon over it and shoved it in the oven. He then gathered the garbage, including the residue from the fish. He took the bag containing the fishy contents, neatly tied up, out to the trunk of his car. In the morning he would take it to the garbage dump.

By supper time Anne had calmed down enough to think a bit about her situation. She did have an entry ticket for tomorrow's bingo. She had won it at a game they had attended in July, as a result of being seated on the left side of someone that had called out "bingo." She knew she wouldn't feel right about going while her friend was lying dead, but she did want to go. It was too late now to make tonight's mini-bingo, but if she left early in the morning, she could be in Yorkton by ten for the big one.

With the decision made to go to Yorkton, she thought about her good-luck charm. She would need that, but after the last game they had attended, Lucille had taken their charms. She had no doubt put them in a drawer somewhere for safe keeping. So in spite of her vow not to enter the place again, she realized she would have to go and get her charm. Well, it should be okay now as she knew Harry was home. She had seen him drive past their house to park in the vacant lot across the back lane from his own dwelling. Later she had seen him come out and put something in his car that looked like a garbage bag. She thought it strange that he was home at all at a time like this. Wasn't there something he should be doing?

He had just taken the fish out of the oven when Anne came in the back door. *Blasted woman never bothers to knock*, thought Harry while at the same time saying, "I thought you girls were on your way to Yorkton." Anne burst out in tears. "Oh my God, you mean you don't know! Haven't you been told yet? Our poor Lucille, someone killed her. Who would do such a thing? And that dear girl so looking forward to the monster bingo in Yorkton. I just can't believe it."

When Harry took the message off the answering machine, there was a number to call. It was the Royal Canadian Mounted Police detachment. A few minutes later, the police were at the Welks' door. They offered condolences, but said they would have to ask him a few questions.

It was noted that Harry had taken the afternoon off from his job at the bank. Why? Where had he spent the afternoon? He told them about working on the antique car with his friend Jake Meyer. They had wanted to get it finished as Jake and his wife were going away for the weekend. Yes, he had been there all afternoon. Harry would later regret that statement.

The police did not question him any further, but made a mental note of what he was having for supper. They told him the body could be released to the funeral home of his choice, any time the next day. The police then left Harry to his salmon supper.

In the morning, before he went to the funeral home in Moose Jaw, Harry stopped at the dump and got rid of the smelly garbage in his trunk. A plain clothes policeman in an unmarked car watched him. When Harry was gone, the policeman dumped the contents of the garbage bag and retrieved the rest of the cello wrap that the fish had been in. He put the wrap in a bag and marked it "Exhibit B."

On Monday morning the police went to the Crown Prosecutor with the evidence they had against Harry Welks. One: Harry had expressed a desire to be rid of his wife. Two: he had asked Jake Meyer to provide him with an alibi as to his whereabouts while his wife was being murdered. Three: when asked where he was that afternoon, Harry had lied to the police. Four: two neighbors would testify that Harry's car had been parked in the driveway at about the time his wife died. Five: there was no sign of forced entry, even though some dresser drawers were messed up. This appeared to be only an attempt by the murderer to make robbery seem to be the motive. Six: Harry had also disposed of the murder weapon. Seven: the only fingerprints found at the scene of the crime, were those of Harry and Lucille.

Bud, although not a smart man, had been careful not to leave his fingerprints. He had entered through the front door, with Lucille opening and closing it. He had opened the deep freeze with the back of his knuckles. The cello wrap on the fish warmed enough in his hands to make moisture that would run and then when froze again left an unreadable print. The last person to handle the telephone was Lucille, so only her prints were evident. When leaving Bud had used his baseball cap to handle the door knob—he had seen that little trick in a movie once.

The Crown Prosecutor told the police to go and place Harry under arrest for the murder of Lucille Welks.

Chapter 12

Tudor, Saskatchewan

Lucille was laid to rest at one-thirty Monday afternoon amid strong winds and squalls of rain. Those in attendance were still in shock that such a terrible thing could have happened in their quiet little community.

Monday evening, having given time for the funeral proceedings to be completed, the police headed for the Welks' home in Tudor to carry out the Crown Prosecutor's order.

Meanwhile, as Harry watched the six o'clock news that evening, several thoughts were going through his head. Had the gods of fate played a role in removing Lucille from his life? Who had killed her? Some transient perhaps! The police would likely catch him. If that came to pass, Harry would be tempted to thank the guy. He also wondered if he should have told the police the truth, about where he was that Friday afternoon. Maybe he would still go to them and change his story.

Harry was paying little attention to the news, but when the weather report was given he noted that seven centimeters of snow had fallen in Saskatoon. It was at this point he heard a rap on the door. When he opened the door to the two policemen standing there, he noticed the rain had turned to snow.

They identified themselves as Corporal Steven Stenowski and Constable Ernest Johnson. "Are you Henry Alfred Welks?" they asked.

"Yes, but most people call me Harry," he replied.

Stenowski said, "We have a warrant for your arrest for first degree murder in the death of Lucille Lavina Welks. You have the right to remain silent, anything you say can be used against you in a court of law . . ."

Harry went quietly, in a state of confusion. They allowed him to put on a coat, cap, and galoshes before placing him in handcuffs. While this was all a new experience for Harry, he was not surprised at the handcuffs, but his own two hands were not cuffed together as he thought they might be. Any newscast he had ever seen of a prisoner being escorted by police always showed the prisoner's hands cuffed in front of him. Harry had no reason to know the exact procedure, but it made little difference to him as one cuff was placed on his right wrist, and the other one on the left wrist of Officer Johnson, thus tying them together. Harry didn't know why but it made him think of the three-legged races, from the school sports days. It was in this formation that he was led to the police cruiser. Approaching the cruiser on the passenger side, Harry was told to get into the back seat, with Johnson getting in beside him. Stenowski drove.

The highway between Regina and Moose Jaw is the Trans-Canada, a double lane divided highway paralleling the railroad. From Regina west-bound, the road is on the south side of the rail line, then a short distance west of Tudor the highway crosses the railroad on a dual S-shaped overpass, then continues west, on the north side of the rails.

As a result of the new fallen snow packing into ice, it was on the west-bound overpass that a small compact car had gone out of control, hitting an overpass railing before flipping over on its side. A semi-trailer was next in line. The driver, trying to avoid hitting the car, also struck the railing, knocking chunks of cement to the rail line below. The trailer portion of the rig had then careened sideways, striking the overturned car, completely blocking the road.

This was the scene that greeted the police as they came up on the overpass. Cpl. Stenowski took charge, being experienced in such matters. He immediately tried to radio for help, but couldn't raise anyone. He ordered Johnson to remain at the accident site and help any of the injured in whatever way he could. Stenowski would go back to the foot of the bridge, or to the first intersection, to set up a road-block. He would have to prevent any more traffic from coming up on the bridge. At the same time he would keep calling in to the detachment for help.

Police cruisers do not have handles on the inside of the back doors, so the Corporal had to step out and go around to the passenger side to open the back door for Johnson before he left. While Stenowski was doing this, Constable Johnson unlocked the cuff from his own wrist, so that he would be free to attend the accident victims without having Harry attached to him.

Johnson got out of the car and Harry got out right behind him, with the loose cuff dangling from his right arm. It was easy enough for him to do this as the attention of the two policemen was directed at the accident scene, rather than on Harry.

The police did not intend to have their prisoner out of the cruiser until they could move him safely into a jail cell. Stenowski, realizing what Harry had done, was about to order him into the back seat again, but thought better of it. He quickly decided that even a prisoner might be after to offer assistance where needed in this, an emergency situation. Further, even though escape from the back seat of the cruiser, with no inside handles was a remote possibility, it was a no-no to leave a prisoner unattended, and unattended he might be as Stenowski set up a road block. And so it was that Harry was left there with Johnson at the accident scene.

At this time of year, darkness falls about six o'clock or a bit later. It was now six-thirty. With the overcast sky, it was completely dark. Johnson quickly took stock. The big truck was on its wheels with the motor running. The driver was unhurt. It was hard to tell about the little car, but no one inside seemed to be moving.

The truck driver got an extension light from his storage box, and when he plugged it into the cigarette lighter they could then see what they were dealing with. The lone occupant of the car had not been wearing a seat belt and his head had struck the windshield. He was unconscious and bleeding badly. The door on the top side of the overturned car could not be opened as a result of the damage done by the impact of the big rig.

Johnson thought if they could get the little car on its wheels, they could get to the injured occupant and maybe get the flow of blood stopped. Johnson and the truck driver tried to lift the car upright manually. They couldn't quite do it. "Hey, Welks—get over here and give us a hand," Johnson bellowed. "Sure," replied Harry, "I'll do whatever I can." The three of them were indeed able to lift the car back on its wheels.

When Harry stepped out of the cruiser behind Johnson, he had no thought of trying to escape, but a seed of thought began to grow in his mind. One thing he knew for sure, he had not killed Lucille. Would justice prevail and exonerate him of the false charges? There were some cases where there had been a miscarriage of justice. A number of cases had made the news, but up until now Harry had paid scant attention to the details.

There was that case that made headlines just this past summer. It had to do with Simon Crowchild, an Indian from a reserve somewhere in Alberta. The Indian had been convicted of murdering a policeman about ten years ago, and now after another Indian from the same reserve had confessed to the crime, Crowchild was found innocent, and released.

It came out in the second trial that the real perpetrator had bragged, while boozing it up with some friends, as to how he had gotten rid of Simon. "Teach him not to mess with my wife." Besides that he had fixed that cop, so he wouldn't be taking another driver's licence from anyone just because they'd had a couple of drinks.

Had Bud Soelen followed that story, and decided to copycat the Indian that had the unfaithful wife? *Unlikely, Bud wouldn't have enough brains to mastermind a scheme like that.*

Another one that came to Harry's mind was about a fourteen year old kid in Ontario, what was his name? Brian someone, yes, Brian Turner. In that case the sentence was to "hang by your neck until you are dead." The sentence was later changed to life in prison. Some woman had written a book on the Turner case, producing evidence as to the boy's innocence and stating that he was a victim of the "system." The part that Harry remembered most about the Turner kid, was that he was the same age as himself.

Harry also wondered about how he would pay for a lawyer. He remembered reading the debate over abolishment of capital punishment in the House of Commons, the former Prime Minister, John Diefenbaker, was quoted as saying, "I have never known a rich man to hang." Harry was not a rich man. He knew, if convicted, he would not hang, as capital punishment had been abolished, but he would find being behind bars for the rest of his life a pill that wouldn't be much easier to swallow.

So it was that when Harry saw the light of a train coming from the east, he pictured his escape. If he made a clean getaway, he would somehow start a new life. Just as he had planned with Irma once they were free of their spouses. However, it was now unlikely there would be any future with Irma. If he didn't make his escape good, the charge of escaping custody would be added to the charge he was already facing but at this point it was not likely to make much difference.

He knew the train was slowing down as he could hear the brakes squealing and the car couplings rattling as the cars bumped ahead on one another. The train crew had probably been warned of the falling cement. So while Johnson and the truck driver were doing what they could for the injured chap in the little car, Harry slipped over the bridge railing and down the grade to the rail tracks. He was then under the bridge and out of sight.

Harry recalled stories his dad had told him of riding the rods during the Great Depression. Who would have ever guessed those old stories would come in handy in a real life situation? Dad always said, "Never grab a boxcar from a standing position, always run as fast as you can beside the train and made a grab for the ladder on the front corner of the car. Never grab the ladder at the rear or you will be thrown between the cars where you could be killed." Many times his Dad had told him a story that he said had actually taken place. It was back in the days when the locomotives pulling the trains were powered by steam, so they had to stop to take on water at various places along the line. There was one such place somewhere west of Moose Jaw that was reported to be the best source between Winnipeg and Calgary. It was while the train was taking on water that one of the "railroad bums" decided he would have time to run over to the store in the little town that was adjacent to the water tower. Perhaps he wanted some cigarettes, or maybe a packet of bologna. Anyway, when he got back the train was already moving at a pretty good pace. He almost missed but was able to grab the ladder of the last box car just ahead of the caboose. His body was thrown between the box car and caboose. He lost his grip and fell, the caboose ran over one leg, severing it just above the knee. That was when the trains were made up with the last car being the caboose, and its only occupant was a member of the train crew called the "brakee." Why he didn't see the fellow and stop the train can only be guessed at, but the train did not stop. The person that saw him and came to his rescue was the cinder man.

The steamers, of course, burned coal to heat the water to make the steam. When the train stopped for water the ashes or cinders were released into a windrow between the rails. The cinder man's job was to load the cinders and wheel them away. When the cinder man saw the guy with the severed leg, he knew he had to do something. The leg was still hanging on by a bit of flesh, so he took out his jackknife and cut the remaining flesh. With his shoelace, he made a tourniquet to stop the flow of blood. Next Mr. Cinder Man contacted the only person in town that had a car. Together they got the guy into the car and took him to a hospital in Moose Jaw. Frank Welks didn't know what had happened after that, but in telling the story he would make mention about the fuss there would be if anything like that happened today. Investigations with no end would be called for. Everyone within hailing distance would be questioned. What was he doing boarding a freight? What were the train crew doing? Was the fellow that severed that last bit of flesh and made the tourniquet a qualified surgeon? The press would have a heyday in today's world of electronic media reporting. Then Frank would always say, "But I guess in those days, one railroad bum more or less didn't make much difference."

As this story and others flashed through his mind Harry prepared to board the freight. He let the engine and a few cars go by, then he ran. He estimated the train was going about four times as fast as he was, because four cars went by as he traveled the length of one. *No use waiting,* he thought, as he grabbed the front ladder of the next car to go by. He knew his grip would have to be firm, and it was. It felt as if his arms would be pulled out of their sockets as his feet left the ground. His body swung to an almost horizontal position, before swinging back again like a pendulum on a clock. He then got a toe on the bottom rung of the ladder. Now to climb to the top of the car. As he was about to ascend, he noted the loose handcuff was dangling right against the rung below the one he had the grip on. What if that thing caught on a rung as he tried to climb, or worse yet the damn thing could hook a rung and snap itself shut again. What a fix that would be, he couldn't take any chances.

His first thought on how to take care of the situation was to simply snap the cuff into a locked position, but after a couple of tries he decided it must have to be locked with a key, as well as unlocked. Well something had to be done, so he let go with the cuffed hand and raised it till the loose cuff was level with his mouth, then grabbed it with his teeth. It reminded him of bobbing for apples, only the cuff was cold and would probably blister his tongue. Without incident he now climbed to the top of the car.

With the wind and snow, he knew he couldn't stay there very long. He inched his way along the top, to the rear of the car, where he was able to jump to a flatcar, loaded with lumber. He scraped and bruised his knee when he landed but considered himself lucky to be alive. The taste of freedom was exhilarating.

The timbers on the flatcar were of uneven length, making a sort of ladder formation. Harry worked his way as far down the icy load as he could, near the front of the flatcar. The boxcar ahead gave him some protection from the cold wind.

It was then Harry started to give some thought to the handcuff dangling from his right arm. He was glad the police had allowed him to put on his winter coat. Not only glad for its warmth but the cuffs on it were snug fitting, and of a woven material that would expand. So with his left hand Harry was able to work the loose handcuff up under the coat cuff of his right arm. By holding his arm up and pushing at the handcuff he got it up to the inside of his elbow joint. Then by pulling the coat cuff over the still locked handcuff he had it concealed.

Chapter 13

Moose Jaw, Saskatchewan

As the train approached the Moose Jaw rail yards and started to slow down, Harry knew he would need some other means of transportation. There was sure to be a welcoming committee if he rode into the yards. He was familiar with this area. He had often played here as a kid when his parents visited friends in Moose Jaw.

The Moose Jaw Creek originated some fifty miles southeast of Moose Jaw and flows northwest into the city. It then makes an abrupt turn to the right, then flows straight east for a couple of miles before it starts angling to the northeast. It is believed by historians that the city got its name from the shape of the outcropping of land that the creek surrounds, as it makes the turn to flow east. The flow coming from the south-east is at about a thirty-five to forty degree angle to the portion that flows east, thus forming a land area that resembles the shape of the jaw of a moose.

Perhaps, when the first white people saw it, there may have been some native willow growing at the right place to resemble the antlers of a moose, there may have been a pool of stagnant water along the shoreline to resemble an eye. There is also a story about some guy with an oxcart and a broken wheel who made the necessary repairs with a bone from the jaw of a moose. Most historians regard the oxcart theory as the figment of someone's imagination.

The main line of the Canadian Pacific railway is built parallel and along the north bank of the creek as it flows east. The double lane Trans-Canada highway alternate route enters the city's east end, then goes in a southwest direction until it reaches the railroad. From there it makes a turn and parallels the railroad and travels straight west, until it makes a junction with number two highway, a north to south road that passes through the city.

The natural terrain on which the city is built slopes towards the creek from both the north and south outer edges of town, so it is only natural that the north part is referred to as North Hill, while the south is called South Hill.

There is yet another rail line that passes through the city, a branch line of the Canadian National Railroad enters the city on North Hill. As the terrain drops, the road bed rises, thus keeping the rail tracks level. When the line reaches the highway alternate it is built on trestles that take the line across the well above the two lanes of the highway alternate, two sets of rail tracks, and the Moose Jaw Creek. It then proceeds on south with the grade decreasing as the terrain rises toward South Hill. To cross the southeast to northwest portion of the creek, it is again on trestles before leaving the city to serve the towns and villages south of Moose Jaw.

As the train with Harry aboard approached the outskirts of the city, Harry knew he would have to make plans. He would need to get off the train before it entered the rail yards, he would also need to get off where there were no roads leading up to a level crossing. Again the words of his dad went through his mind in regard to riding the rods. "Always face the same direction as the train is going and land on your feet running if you can." He vacated the train with no problem. The next thing was to get as far away from the rail line as he could, and get out of Moose Jaw as quickly as he could. He had read lots of news stories where some fugitive of the law tried to hole up in a house in town, and was either flushed out with tear gas, or just talked into giving himself up.

A plan for a way out of town started to develop. He knew from the cheques processed at the bank that there were loads of cattle leaving for Ontario or the United States almost on a daily basis. If there were one leaving between now and daylight tomorrow, he would try to be in with the cattle.

To get to the stockyards he would have to get to South Hill. The water in the creek was likely low enough, but to get through the willow growth on the creek banks in the dark and in this storm, would be next to impossible. There were streets that crossed the Pacific rail line, by means of an overpass, also some with an underpass. To try it on one of them would be tantamount to giving himself up.

As a kid he had often walked on the rail line that was built high up on those trestles. The kids involved generally got a good scolding or sometimes they got their backsides warmed for the practice. It was dangerous, they were told, and Harry guessed it was. Still, it was the route he would choose now whether it was dangerous or not. He got away from the train and onto the west bound lane of the alternate, better time could be made on the pavement than in the ditch.

There was no traffic, and if something came along he would make for the ditch. Something did come by and it was more than he had planned on. A truck appeared on the east bound lane with a search-light sweeping the ditches. *What to do?* Luck was with him, a tarp had blown off somebody's truck and was lying in the ditch between the two lanes. Harry made a jump from the shoulder of the road to the tarp, so as not to leave footprints. He was able to get under the tarp, but then frantically thought that maybe whoever lost the tarp was back looking for it. The truck never stopped, so as soon as it was gone Harry heaved a sigh of relief and was back on the pavement running west. He would have to keep going, as he would need to get through the underpass of the alternate. Once he was on the west side of the rail line he could climb the shoulder and get on the rails that would take him across to South Hill. The east side would have quite a bit of snow accumulation by now, making a climb up that side very difficult. Without seeing any more traffic, he made it through the underpass, then went north for a couple of blocks, where the climb up the bank would not be as steep. Harry was now on his way to South Hill and some twenty feet above the railroad he had just left.

As he made the crossing he could see people with high powered flashlights well to the west of him, and Harry thought, *As long as they concentrate their efforts in that area I'll be okay.* Even if one of them did shine a light toward Harry as he made his way across the overpass they wouldn't see him in the swirling snow.

After the rail line crossed the creek, the most adjacent buildings were those of the Moose Jaw Sportsman's Center, a place Harry knew well, as he often spent some time there. This time he never called in, but instead skirted the parking lot and headed west towards the stock-yards. He knew he had close to a mile to go, but by staying out of the lighted areas and keeping mostly to back alleys, he got to where he could see the loading ramps of the stockyards. Luck was with him, there was a cattle liner backing up to a loading ramp.

Harry waited in the shadows until the driver and his helper had gone inside the sheds. He made a run for it and settled down on his knees at the front of the upper level of the cattle transport. Ten minutes later, cattle were herded into the unit. The first ones in sniffed at Harry, but showed no alarm. After the cattle were loaded, a flashlight shone in over the cattle but Harry was not spotted in his kneeling position. The end gates were closed and before long the truck was moving. Harry stood up in a more comfortable position where he was more likely to avoid being covered in excrement.

Harry was glad the walk-up ramp to the cattle liner was positioned for the upper level. Anyone looking through the holes into the upper level would have to stand on a ladder or climb the side, to be able to see inside. Standing in the moving truck, he started to scratch the back of the animal closest to him. The animal seemed to like it and Harry thought, *Well, little critter, neither of us know where we are going, but it is going to be a long night.*

At times Harry was able to doze a bit, but was fully awake when the truck came to a full stop. He was able to see through the holes that they were at the junction of Highway 13 and Highway 39, just west of Weyburn. He also noted it had quit snowing. It did not look as if there had been any snow here at all. When the truck continued on through Weyburn, he knew they were on Highway 39, likely heading for the "Corn State" of Iowa. They would be crossing the border into the States at the North Portal crossing, less than one hour away.

The exchange between the driver and the Customs official lasted less than two minutes, and they were moving again.

Chapter 14

Moose Jaw, Saskatchewan

When Constable Johnson realized that Harry had slid down the embankment and onto the railway tracks under the bridge, he drew his revolver and peered into the darkness. Johnson could hear the train and thought Harry would never get away anyway. All Harry would get for his efforts would be a cold ride into Moose Jaw, when he could have been comfortable in the back seat of the cruiser.

With his cell phone Johnson called the Moose Jaw RCMP detachment. They, in turn, notified the Moose Jaw city police. Between the two forces a welcoming committee of twelve officers was on hand to greet Harry when he arrived at the rail yards. Cars were covering each approach leading up to the rail line.

When Harry didn't appear, roadblocks were immediately set up on all highways leading out of Moose Jaw. Hundreds of cars were stopped during the next eighteen hours. Even the most innocent looking vehicles were stopped, very few were waved through without a search. One that did get through was the cattle liner carrying Harry, who didn't even realize there was a roadblock.

Some of the drivers inconvenienced by the roadblocks got quite indignant. The police had no right to stop them and they were late already as a result of the storm. Three drivers were given twenty-four hour suspensions for driving under the influence of drugs or alcohol. The police did not have the resources to take them into custody and charge them with impaired driving.

Brian and Nancy Billings were part of a ring that had found out they could make good money kidnapping children and then selling them. There was a lucrative market in some parts of the world, and it was much safer than kidnapping for ransom. As the stores were closing for the day, Brian and Nancy had some bags outside a supermarket. Ten-year-old Adam Southby had been in the video arcade. When he came out, the Billings couple asked him if he would help them carry their groceries to their car. They offered him a dollar for his help.

When they got to the car, Nancy opened the back door and Brian slipped a needle through Adam's coat and into his left arm. He collapsed in a matter of seconds, and was shoved into the back seat. In less than two minutes the Billings, with Adam, were on the road.

When they were stopped at the road block on Highway #1 East, Constable David Hart, in his second year with the RCMP, asked the usual questions. Where did they come from, where were they going, asked to see Brian's driver's licence and vehicle registration. They said they had left Calgary that morning with plans to go as far as Winnipeg, but with the weather the way it was, they would only go as far as Regina. Hart noticed the boy in the back seat and made the comment, "Your boy looks to have made a day of it already."

"Yes," replied Nancy, "he has had two big days playing with his cousins in Calgary."

Another car was approaching, so the Billings were sent on their way. Something about that car with the Ontario licence plate bothered Hart; that kid in the back seat did not appear to be in a natural sleep.

Just before David Hart went off duty, a report came in that a ten-year-old boy was missing from Moose Jaw. The description seemed to fit that of the boy in the Ontario car. Hart was glad he had made a note of the licence plate number, and did not hesitate to call into headquarters with his suspicions.

The Billings were again stopped east of Winnipeg, and this time they were taken into custody. Adam Southby was returned to his parents in Moose Jaw. Once the Southby family heard the story of the roadblocks and the escape of the fugitive Harry Welks, they thanked their lucky stars for giving them Welks. They secretly hoped he would escape and never be found.

It took over a year, but the Billings and five of their colleagues were convicted and sentenced for their efforts. Meanwhile, the roadblocks revealed no clue as to the whereabouts of the fugitive and the house to house search in Moose Jaw was to no avail. However, the search did turn up some interesting situations that changed people's relationships forever.

Patrolman Warren Woodrow was the son of an Anglican priest and had at one time studied theology. He gave it up, and with his best friend Edgar Trimble joined the city police force. Edgar married a lovely girl from Swift Current, while Warren had remained single and lived with his parents who appreciated the help and the rent money he contributed.

Warren was called in on his day off, the night Harry Welks escaped. He was working alone equipped with a two-way radio. Should any clue regarding Harry turn up, the instructions were to radio for help rather than try to apprehend him alone.

Warren had been plodding through the snow in the back alleys. He had been checking old buildings and knocking on doors for about three hours. He was cold and miserable as he passed the alley behind his friend Edgar's place. He knew Edgar was at work and his wife Peggy was likely in bed, but Warren decided to enter the house by the back door and make himself a quick cup of coffee, as he often did. The Trimbles had always made him welcome, so he easily made himself at home.

Warren did not feel that a short break would be shirking his duty, and anyway, he should warn Peggy to keep her doors locked. He didn't knock on the back porch door, because Peggy would never hear him anyway. The door was unlocked as usual. He rapped on the door leading to the kitchen a couple of times, then opened the door, hollering, "Anybody home?" No answer, he didn't expect one on the first call. It was only seconds after he turned on the kitchen light that a nude figure dashed out of the bedroom and across the front room to the front door. It was a male and he had some clothes clutched in his hand. As he opened the front door, Warren recognized the interloper as the next door neighbor of the Trimbles. Warren said, "You had better take time to put your clothes on, you shouldn't go out on a night like this dressed as you are." He did quickly slip into his pants and shoes before going down the front steps.

Warren hardly knew what he should do. Maybe he should quietly leave, but Peggy must know he was there and what he had seen. He abandoned the idea of coffee and just plugged in the kettle. When it got hot he would throw a tea bag into a cup. If Peggy showed herself, okay, if not, he would just leave.

By the time the water was hot Peggy did come out dressed in a housecoat and yawning as if just awakened. They both knew it was a phony act. The housecoat was open enough at the top so that Warren could tell she had nothing on under it.

Conversation was strained, Warren told her about the escaped Harry Welks. Peggy toyed with the idea of offering to let Warren finish what the neighbor had started. A reward like that might ensure his silence. However, she dropped the idea after considering Warren's upbringing. The Woodrow family still lived by the golden rule and followed the Ten Commandments. Warren finished his tea and told Peggy he had to go back to work.

He never mentioned the incident to Edgar, but visits by Warren to the Trimble home became less frequent and the jovial chatter all but disappeared. Edgar never understood why, but guessed Warren was finding other interests. He was right. Warren resigned from the police force the following spring, and again took up the study of theology. It was eventually his destiny to go to India as a missionary.

As the days following Harry's escape stretched into a week, then two, there were numerous reports of him being spotted in many parts of the country. Someone saw him getting on a Greyhound bus in North Battleford. He was spotted in an airport in Vancouver. Another saw him in a supermarket in Sudbury, Ontario.

All of these leads had to be followed up with an investigation. Someone in Edmonton about Harry's age reported having his passport stolen, and someone by the same name was reported to have bought an airline ticket to Puerto Vallarto, Mexico. A follow-up on the Mexican trip showed the purchaser to be an eighty-two-year-old man who made the same trip every year. He was a member of a group known as snowbirds, who went south every year to escape the Canadian winters.

Crime Stoppers ran their usual TV ads, indicating they would pay up to two thousand dollars for information that would lead to the arrest of Harry Welks, or any of their other outstanding cases.

A woman from Regina phoned Crime Stoppers to tell them she knew where to find Harry Welks. She wanted the money first and then she would tell. It was explained to her that she could be charged with obstruction of justice if she had vital information and chose to withhold it. She wanted to know when she would get the money and how could she be sure she would get it. After a bit of haggling, she gave them the address of a Regina home where, according to her, she had seen Harry come and go on more than one occasion. The search turned up nothing.

As the media gained more information about the case, it was released that the murder weapon had been a frozen fish. The fish had since been eaten by the accused Harry Welks.

Dozens of letters were written to the editor of the local newspaper. Some with a bit of humor.

The Federal Minister of Justice was introducing a bill that would require all owners of firearms to keep them under lock and key, except when in use. The bill would also require ammunition to be stored in a separate place, also under lock and key. The bill was not very popular in the West, so one writer to the editor suggested that since frozen fish had been found to be a lethal weapon, the law should require them to be under lock and key as well. Since the fins were the lethal portion, they should be removed and stored separately.

Lots of letters offered opinions as to how Harry had escaped. None suggested a cattle liner. One thought he had got himself arrested under an assumed name and was now safely in jail until the heat died down. Another thought he had outside help and had been crated, as some kind of a "started" variety of apple tree that would do well in the north, and had been shipped to the Yukon.

Apart from the actual culprit, there was one person who knew for sure Harry had not murdered Lucille. While the big slob was getting herself murdered, Harry was spending the afternoon in a motel room with Irma Soelen. Should she go to the police with her story? Would they believe her? *No,* she thought, *best to stay silent unless Harry is apprehended. Who did kill Lucille? Could it have been some transient?* Irma remembered a case where a couple of women had been murdered by a transient in a little town in Manitoba. The weapon had been a broomstick. The transient had no connection with the women at all, he just killed them because he thought all society was against him. He had been found innocent of murder on the grounds of insanity, and was committed to a mental institution. Someday he would be released as cured. Could this be a similar situation?

Irma also wondered if her husband Bud was in some way involved. He had never liked Harry and when the news broke about the murder, Bud was quick enough to comment that they wouldn't have to look very far for the murderer. Irma did, in a discrete sort of way, question some of Bud's drinking buddies to find out it they had seen Bud on that fatal Friday afternoon. She never came out with a point blank question, like "Are you sure?" but it did seem Bud had spent the entire day in the bar.

The police had several questions for Jake Myer, since he had notified Crime Stoppers that Harry had asked Jake to provide an alibi for him during the time of the murder. Jake told the police that Harry had said he had spent the afternoon with Irma Soelen, the two had planned to run away together as soon as he got rid of Lucille.

The police did not question Irma, instead they tapped her phone. Irma thought they may have done this, as one day when Jake was in the café he mentioned that the police had called on him, and if she had any idea where Harry was, she should tell them.

Irma knew that wherever Harry was, he would never try to phone or write to her. A letter could be intercepted and read by Bud. It did occur to her that if her phone was bugged, she would give them some gossip worth listening to.

She became quite innovative at creating stories about several of the town's leading citizens. When she was talking to one of her friends, she would always start out the conversation saying, "Don't let this go any further, but there were some people in the café today. I just heard bits of the conversation but I gathered that . . ." then would come a story she had made up. The police chief was involved in a drug ring, the mayor was having an affair with his secretary, a school principal was molesting little boys. She would never say enough to bring about a charge of libel, but she sure started some vicious rumors. By the time the stories had been repeated a few times, no one knew their origin. Without knowing it, Harry had guided the hand of fate and changed the path of the lives of a great many people.

While Harry wouldn't write to her, Irma did think he might try to contact her through the personal column of some newspaper. She became one of the best customers at the local newsstand. Not only did she buy copies of local papers, but also bought papers from cities all across the country. *The Vancouver Sun, The Edmonton Journal, The Globe and Mail,* and even one from Dauphin, Manitoba. This search of the personal columns ran into weeks without even a hint of a message from Harry. She wished she could reach him so they could decide what to do. If he gave himself up she would go to court on his behalf.

As time went on and the search of personal columns revealed nothing, Irma decided to run some ads herself, hoping that Harry would read them.

On that Friday afternoon when they had been in the motel room, they had started to make plans for the future. Harry was sure he could get a job with the Dauphin, Manitoba branch of the bank. Irma could likely land a waitress job anywhere. This was Irma's reason for buying the Dauphin newspaper.

For Irma to make the break, they decided all she would have to do was to walk out on Bud. They were glad there were no children in either situation.

The break up of Harry and Lucille would not be as simple, the courts had a way of treating a broken-hearted wife generously. They agreed not to be seen together publicly until after the divorce settlement was made. They thought it would go better for Harry if there wasn't another woman involved.

As they worked out their plan of action, they had developed a code system as a means of contacting each other. They called it their "plus one-minus two system." It went like this. The person sending the message would decide what to say and then scramble the message by changing the first character in the message by moving it one ahead, this would apply whether it was a letter of the alphabet or a number. The second character in the message would be moved two backward. The third character one ahead and so on. So if the message was to read I LOVE YOU, the letter I would become a J, the letter L would become a J, the letter O becomes a P and so on until the entire message would read J JPTF WPS. The person doing the unscrambling would reverse the procedure by making it, minus one-plus two.

So Irma created her message for the personal column and it read, J JJJM GFJQ WPS CNZ 653 JPNY. If Harry should see it and un-scramble the message it would read, I WILL HELP YOU BOX 734 IRMA.

To start with, she just put the ad in the local paper. She could not fill in the box number until she rented one from the newspaper. She rented the reply box for two weeks. If he saw the ad he would use the city and the postal code of the paper the ad was in.

The clerk taking the ad wondered what kind of a nut this was, wanting gibberish like that in the paper. *She doesn't even have the box number right, what a fool.* The clerk shrugged her shoulders and thought, *Who am I to care what she writes?*

Irma never got a reply to this or any other ad she had placed, but she suspected the curiosity of a few people was piqued.

Chapter 15

Saigon, Vietnam

After a couple of stops for refueling, the troop carrier arrived at the airport in Saigon. The troops were immediately taken to a camp thirty miles outside Saigon, where there was more military training in the jungles of Vietnam.

In the army, regardless of the walk of life a person comes from they all have one thing in common. They are about the same age. These men of the same age group make friends quickly. Some friends are closer than others. Some friendships formed in the army last a lifetime. One fellow that Jack hit it off with was a chap from the state of Maryland, by the name of George Shipley. George was not married, but he did talk about his mother and two sisters back home from time to time, but he never said much else about his background.

George Shipley had always been an embarrassment to his family. He had held a number of part-time jobs, a dishwasher in a restaurant, Santa Claus in a department store. The only full time job he had ever had was with a funeral home. A job he held for two years, and it had pleased the family no end when it seemed he had found a vocation that he was suited for, and readily adapted to. However, George found out there were a few dollars to be picked up on the side. This was accomplished by removing any jewelry the departed had planned on taking with them to the great beyond. He was smart enough to know he couldn't just remove a ring, for example, and leave that white band of skin where the ring had been for the bereaved to see. George took care of this by picking up imitation products at Woolworth's to replace the one of value he had removed.

Really what harm was done, as the departed look quite natural lying there with such peaceful poses on their faces. What was more, the departed never complained. This all came to an end when a gentleman of some means came to view the remains of his beloved wife of over fifty years. As he took a closer look at the gold band he had given her those many years ago, he saw that it somehow seemed different. To satisfy himself he asked the undertaker to remove the ring, saying that he had decided it should be handed down in the family a an heirloom. On looking for the engraving that should have been on the inside, he noticed that it was not there. He had taken such pains to get it just right, "To Gloria—with all my love, Philip" the words had said. On pointing the matter out to the undertaker, it was soon determined that George had removed the ring. George explained his actions by saying he thought the husband would be glad to have the ring back as a keepsake, and the replacement looked just as natural. Yes, he had dropped the ring in a drawer with some embalming tools until there was a chance to return it.

When it couldn't be found, a search of pawn shops was made, and it did not take long to find and identify it. The pawnbroker also readily identified George, because George had a face like none other. He bore a mass of pockmarks, from having had measles as a kid, and as he couldn't refrain from scratching the pustules, the pockmarks left him permanently scarred. After losing the job with the funeral home, the next move was to join the army. He was not drafted, but had enlisted on a voluntary basis. The Vietnam war was winding down, and it looked to him that the army would be a life of luxury. Perhaps he might be sent somewhere on the other side of the world as part of a peacekeeping force.

The troops settled into a regular routine and after a month they were all given a forty-eight hour pass. Jack and his buddy George went into Saigon. For the life of him, Jack just couldn't understand what this war was all about. Who would give their life to defend this God-forsaken land? Jack wouldn't trade one square foot of his five acres at Bismark for the whole damn country.

In Saigon, George seemed to know more about where to go and what to see than Jack. George had probably done some homework. They visited a number of bars and when Jack had enough booze in him to lower his sense of values, George suggested they make a visit to one of the "flesh shops." Jack didn't really think it was right, but George insisted saying, "Hell, come on, it is only those Catholic priests that stay celibate all their life. Besides, if we knew the truth, there are probably some of them who strayed from time to time." They spent the rest of their leave with a couple of Vietnamese women, who were young and very attractive.

Back at camp on Monday, Jack made to vow to himself that when he got home he would make a full confession to Doris. He felt she would understand the pressure he was under and forgive him. He would never do it again.

Still, he did do it again and again, on a regular basis. George was good at forgery, and found out how to create a few extra forty-eight hour passes. George told Jack that he had always had a talent for copying other people's handwriting. He used to play hooky from school and then take a forged note to school the next day, supposedly from his father, explaining his absence. As George put it, he could do his father's signature better than his father could.

The routine continued during the winter of 72–73. The camp was then moved another one hundred miles to the north. The Viet Cong were withdrawing. Sometimes a plane would get by the South Vietnamese resistance and bomb a village. Sometimes the American troops were called in to bury the dead and bring the wounded into camp for medical treatment. Jack wondered if Alan Alda, the start of that new TV series MASH had ever seen anything like this.

◆ ◆ ◆

Back in Bismark, Doris carried on with her job at the dental clinic. Jack had signed over a portion of his army pay, and as this was supplemented by a spouse's allowance, she had almost as much income as when Jack was at home. The times were stressful for her, worrying about the baby and whether Jack was all right.

She watched the war news on TV and read every scrap of news she could find in the papers. She bought maps of Vietnam and she pictured, in her own mind, what the country must look like. She fixed the location of a whole host of towns and villages, which previously had meant nothing to her. Phnom Penh, Loc Nine, Loc Nhi, Of Nang,

Hanoi, and many more. She became familiar with the strange sounding names of their leaders such as Pam Van Dong.

Doris wrote countless letters to Jack and had received only a couple of replies. He didn't tell her much, maybe his letters were censored. It was getting close to the baby's due date, the doctor said she was fine, she hoped the baby would be born on Christmas Day. Then she could write Jack and tell him that they had the best Christmas gift ever.

Doris had mentioned a few times to her parents that she would like to have one of those small European cars to go to work in, as Jack's half ton truck was hard for her to handle and it used a lot of gas. Her dad found a Volvo for sale at the garage where Jack used to work. He bought it and drove it to Bismark for her. Her mother followed in their car. It was agreed that Doris' mother would stay with her until the baby was born, while her father would return home to Williston.

The baby didn't wait until Christmas but arrived at seven in the morning on December 23. He was bright and healthy and Doris named him Robert Hunter Nelson. His middle name, Hunter, was for her grandfather, the late senator. A picture was taken of little Bobby and sent to Jack along with a happy note telling him he was now a father. Doris took a month long maternity leave to be with Bobby.

◆　◆　◆

As the winter progressed, Jack's good buddy George introduced him to marijuana. It was readily available almost anywhere in the villages. After smoking a joint one sure felt relaxed. One needed something to relieve the boredom, and George told Jack that it was a non-addictive substance. You could stop smoking it at any time. Jack felt he was lucky to have a friend like George who was worldly and seemed to know everything.

In March of 1973, one of the biggest offensives by the Viet Cong was launched. There were thousands of them riding in both trucks and tanks, supported by air power. They overran village after village in South Vietnam and slaughtered thousands.

The platoon Jack and George were in was just outside one of the villages the Viet Cong overran. The platoon managed to evade them and then fell in behind. The carnage and mutilation that Jack's platoon witnessed was horrendous. Some said the Viet Cong would toss babies in the air and then catch them on bayonets just for sport.

The few bombings they had previously experienced were child's play compared to this. Peace talks were still ongoing and there were not supposed to be any air strikes from either side.

Once Platoon Sergeant Ashcroft, generally referred to as "Sarge Ash," saw their situation, he ordered the twenty man platoon to fall in behind the Cong. He radioed ahead to the base to warn them. Maybe the Cong would get a taste of their own medicine!

However, nothing went right. Contact with base could not be made. Before they knew what was happening another wave of Viet Cong attacked from the rear. They were surrounded, with machine guns trained on them.

They were forced to march back north about three miles to where a hastily built campground awaited them. They were held in the camp overnight and loaded into trucks the next morning, then taken to a prison camp.

No one slept much that night. Jack Nelson and George Shipley had to get serious about their situation for the first time since arriving in Vietnam. They agreed they should exchange mementos, in case only one of them survived. Then the survivor could take the keepsake back to family members in the States. Jack took off his chain and locket with the picture of Doris and gave it to George. George gave Jack a picture of himself and his two sisters that was taken back in school.

The next morning while they were being loaded into the truck, for the trip to a prison camp, George made a break for it and managed to make it to some bush thirty yards away from the truck, when a guard dropped him with a single shot. They never went to see if he was dead, just loaded the rest of the platoon and drove off.

George wasn't dead but he was bleeding badly. The bullet had entered the fleshy part of his hip and came out in the groin area. He was able to move his leg, so he knew there were no broken bones. He knew he had to stop the bleeding. He was able to crawl far enough into the bush to be out of sight. Then he made it to a fallen tree and thought if he sat on it with some padding over the small hole he could stop the bleeding from the entry wound. The groin wound was much larger, but since he was sitting up he opened his pants and wadded strips of his shirt into the wound. It took most of the forenoon, but the blood finally clotted and stopped flowing. He knew if he moved much it would start bleeding again, so he lay down prone beside the fallen tree and stayed there until nightfall.

Just as it was getting dark, two women found him. They had been foraging for any loot they would find in the aftermath of the battle. They communicated with gestures and loaded him into their hand cart. They took him to a shack that was concealed further back in the bush, where they had escaped the Viet Cong slaughter because nobody had found their hut.

They got George settled on a cot and gave him some tea, but nothing to eat. George was hungry, but what he really wanted was a "joint." He managed to get some sleep off and on during the night, but he was in a lot of pain by morning. The women then brought him a small bowl of rice and some tea. George was not sure what kind of tea it was, but assumed it was a mixture of some kind of herbal remedy.

After a couple of days, the pain had subsided and he was able to move around. He was still unsteady on his feet, but was glad he had not developed a fever. The women gestured that one of them would go to his base camp and get help. This was good news to George, he wrote a note for them to take to the base camp. As he wrote the note he hoped the camp had not been overrun during the charge that had captured his platoon and wrought such havoc on the surrounding villages. George couldn't know it for sure, but the Cong must have done enough damage to meet whatever it was they were wanting to accomplish, because the air-power turned back north after George's friends were taken prisoner. The base camp survived unscathed.

After three weeks in the army hospital in Saigon, George was repatriated back to the States.

Chapter 16

Wives of the M.I.A.

International law requires that prisoners taken in combat give their captors their name, rank, and serial number. The captors in return are required to notify the prisoner's home country of their imprisonment. The Viet Cong did not adhere to any law but their own. No one was ever notified of their capture.

Since there was no record of these men being captured, they were listed as "Missing in Action and Presumed Dead." Doris read the telegram that was delivered by the Department of National Defense in a state of shock and disbelief.

"We regret to inform you that your husband John Ingvald Nelson has been reported missing in action and presumed dead." Doris put the telegram down and vowed there was a mistake. Jack couldn't be dead. He was too young and had too much to live for, he just couldn't be dead. Doris felt it in her soul. Jack was alive.

It was not long before Doris discovered she was not alone. There were other wives who had received the same telegram. One of them lived right in Bismark. Her name was Janice Macabee. Janice and Doris became good friends through their common bond.

They discovered a group called the Wives of the M.I.A. (Missing in Action). Janice and Doris wrote to an address they found in the newspaper. They became active members of the organization and received information on group activities. Their spokespersons appeared on national TV and on open line radio talk shows. They lobbied Congress. The war had officially ended but the Wives of the M.I.A. wanted positive proof that their husbands were dead. Identity of a corpse could be established through dental records. The government of the United States had a responsibility here. They needed to send a team back into Vietnam to conduct a search for casualties or survivors.

Eight months after Doris received that dreadful telegram, she opened the door to see a rather seedy looking specimen of humanity standing there. George Shipley had been thinking of this visit ever since he left Nam. He knew Doris was a good looking woman from the picture in Jack's locket. In person she looked even better. George reasoned that since Doris had been alone for so long, she might appreciate having a man around.

He planned to convince her that Jack was dead and logically, as Jack's best buddy, he would step in and take his place.

He already had a convincing story to tell her. After he introduced himself and gave Doris the locket, he began his story. He told Doris that their platoon had been attacked by the Viet Cong. Jack had both his legs broken and George himself was badly wounded and unable to help his friend. He told her of the two women who had helped him. *At least that part was true*. He said that after he returned to the base camp he helped a search patrol by supplying them with a map of the area where the attack took place. However, all they found were mutilated bodies. Heads had been severed and set on posts. It was well known that the Viet Cong did not take prisoners. He told her he was very sorry to have to tell her these details but felt she had a right to know. To himself he thought, *Jack is probably dead anyway, so what the heck!*

Something about his guy did not sit well with Doris. He was just too forward, especially when he offered to show her his groin wound. She thanked him for returning the locket but said she was still going to continue to support the Wives of the M.I.A. in their efforts to find proof. The skulls from those posts must be somewhere.

She got rid of George Shipley as soon as she could without showing too much disrespect.

Distance and cost prevented Doris and Janice from attending most meetings of the M.I.A., but they did manage to get to one in Chicago. While at the meeting she heard stories from other women who had been approached by men like Shipley. They would have some story of how their husband had died, and as a reward for this information they should jump into bed with the bearer of sad tales.

The warning was, "Girls Beware." Contact the military top brass they served under and see if their stories had any truth to them.

Time passed and it was well into 1974 when some congressman announced he would introduce a Bill to have the "Missing in Action" declared officially dead. This would save the American taxpayer the cost of keeping them on the payroll. After all, it was well over a year since the peace treaty had been signed. If any of the M.I.A. were still alive they would have showed up by now. What it would do was to stop the paycheques that people like Doris were receiving.

The Wives of the M.I.A. put up a storm of protest. Full page ads were placed in newspapers across the country. How could so many people be declared dead without proof? Their motto was PROOF, Please Rely Only On Facts. As a result, the bill was never presented to Congress.

Chapter 17

Prisoners of War

When the platoon of prisoners arrived at their destination, they found they had been taken to a collective farm. They were met and addressed by the farm overseer, who spoke fluent English. He said he had a degree in Agriculture, which he had obtained from a college in the U.S.A. There were about a dozen guards on hand who were armed with rifles confiscated from the American prisoners. The overseer told them his name was Long Ten Dong, and he was in charge. They would be held until the North Vietnamese army removed the government that the people of South Vietnam were forced to endure. Once this was accomplished all the population of Vietnam, both South and North, would live as they pleased, where all people were equal, with no class discrimination. Only then would the war be over. When that time came, he told them, "You will all be released to go back to your own country. You will, of course, be required to give us your names and serial number so that your own country can be advised of your capture." Ash and his men never knew it, but the list of names never left the prison camp.

Mr. Dong then went on to tell them how fortunate they were to be captured by a compassionate people like the Viet Cong. "In some countries you could find yourselves back in battle, and forced to kill your own countrymen. Perhaps to work in a munitions factory, where the results of your labour would be used against your own people. All we ask of you is some honest work in the production of food, food that will be used in our own sustenance as well as that of our fellow man. You will each be allotted daily tasks, and if done well, you may be rewarded with an extra ration from time to time. If your jobs are done in a half hearted measure, there may be some restrictions placed upon you."

After the overseer's speech they thought that perhaps they weren't going to be too badly treated. Jack was sure that if all they wanted out of him was work, he could still do that. They were soon to find out that the reward for extra effort was drugs and alcohol.

For the life of him Ash could not understand why the reward for extra effort was not meat and potatoes, rather than vodka and marijuana. Surely a properly nourished body would put forth more effort in the work place than one that was undernourished and further weakened by drugs.

Maybe he was carrying out some kind of a scientific experiment to determine what the human body could endure. Perhaps he was writing a documentary on the use of the stuff that could be used in sales promotion. One would need to get inside the head of Mr. Dong to know what sort of reasoning went on there. It would seem that his ultimate goal was complete control over the men.

Most of them worked well enough to earn the rewards offered, but this only resulted in them becoming more addicted, as most of them, including Jack, already were. This situation gave Dong a real lever over them. As their bodies developed a craving, all he had to do was cut them off to make them bow to any demand. To add to the abuse of their bodies from the drugs and booze, their diet, which consisted mostly of rice and vegetable broth, didn't do much for them either. Meat was a rarity.

Along with the bribes and awards, the workings of the camp became clear, it was a commune. The grain crops were harvested and went to the common pot of the commune, but the vegetables and the marijuana were a cash crop with the profits going into the pocket of Mr. Dong. Anyone caught stealing vegetables to supplement his diet would pay a heavy price. Sarge Ash didn't like what he was seeing, he was smart enough to resist using any of the marijuana or alcohol himself, he just let Dong thing he was enjoying his generosity. Generally the first thing any prisoner of war would do was try to find some means of escape. In laying out an escape plan, one of the things to consider was the lay of the land adjacent to the camp. They should also try to master as much of the native language as possible. Transportation was another area of concern. Ash knew if they were going to do anything it needed to be done soon. Dong was getting too much control over the men with his drugs, if he suspected any plans to escape he would likely be able to get one of them to talk.

Ash started thinking about it. The language might not make much difference. It would only be useful if they were trying to pass themselves off as part of the native population, quite difficult, as the features of the Orientals were so different from that of Caucasians. There wasn't much opportunity to gain any knowledge of the surrounding terrain, other than the grain fields they had to work in. They would have to get much further than just the perimeters of the grain fields.

Ash would need to take in a confidant, as plans were made for an escape. There was one soldier who had caught the eye of Sergeant Ashcroft ever since boot camp. Ash saw in Jack Nelson the potential for a man who could make a career of military life. Jack carried himself well, marched well, and even after long route marches, he still looked and acted like a soldier. He seemed to enjoy military life. As far as Ash was concerned Jack should already be wearing Corporal stripes. Ash couldn't know it, but Jack hated every minute of army life.

Ash also knew that George Shipley had been a bad influence on Jack, he knew they were messing with drugs. The morning he saw Shipley fall from a single rifle shot he thought, *Good riddance.* He also knew about the forged passes that were probably good enough to get by the military police at the guardhouse entry to camp, but it didn't make them present for roll call on the parade square. If it had only been Shipley, Ash would have marked them AWOL, absent without leave, but rather than get Jack in trouble, he would report to the Battalion Commander, "All present and accounted for." It didn't bother Ash much when he did this, because like Jack he didn't know why any of them were present in this country at all.

So it was to Jack that Ash explained his escape plan. He also extracted a promise from Jack that he would not use any of the vodka or drugs offered. It was a promise that Jack was unable to keep entirely, but he was able to control his actions enough to carry on with his allotted tasks in a satisfactory manner, with his mind still functioning somewhat normally. Ash went over the plans with Jack, and together they looked at them step by step, always looking for a spot that might go wrong, then see if there might be a way around it.

They would need to overpower a guard, then commandeer a vehicle. As they started making plans, it was decided that none of the others would be advised until the time came to put their plan into action. They had already noted that at night there was usually only one guard. He was in a glassed-in tower a short way from the building that housed the prisoners. Since the prison building was kept locked at night, it would take more planning to finalize an escape route out of the prison itself.

Their prison was built of precast cement blocks. A small window installed near the door let in some light, and also enabled the prisoners to look across the compound. The window, of course, had bars over it, making escape by that route out of the question. The compound was also patrolled by a German Shepherd dog at night. It was a habit of the dog that caught the attention of Ash. He noted that at least once a night the dog would cock his leg and urinate against a steel post that supported a floodlight at the front of the building.

Ash did some more thinking, the light on the post must get its power through a live wire that went up inside the hollow post, and would likely be grounded to the post itself. The seeds of a plan that would terminate any problem the dog might cause as the escape took place were starting to germinate.

To set the trap, he was visualizing, a short piece of extension wire would be needed. Attach the extension to the live wire, likely just below the earth surface, then tie the other end to a metal mat for the dog to stand on while he raised his leg. The stream of urine from the dog to the post would complete the circuit, and zappo, one well fried hot dog. If the jolt was strong enough, a breaker would go, and plunge the camp into darkness. *All the better.*

There was a steel mat at the door of their barracks. It was sort of a woven wire thing to scrape their boots on, and it could be rolled up. If placed in the right position under the floodlight, it could work well in his plans. As he visualized what might happen he saw the first problem. The hot wire attached to the matting would short itself through the earth, and blow a circuit before the dog stepped anywhere near, especially with the moisture in the ground from recent rains.

There would have to be insulation of some sort under the mat.

What? When captured most of them were wearing camouflage battle dress, the material was treated with something that made it all but waterproof. Material from some of them would become an insulation sheet to go under the mat, decided Ash.

Ash reasoned that before doing anything about starting various segments of the plan, he should move the mat to the proper position under the flood light. The mat got moved one evening, just after the prisoners returned from the fields. No one seemed to notice the change in its location. The dog still continued as before by stopping each night to dampen the lamp post, only now he did his thing while standing on the mat. Ash was pleased.

Chapter 18

Prison Camp

The next step was to lay plans for a way out of the building. Ash had noticed a lot of cracks in the cement floor. One spot near an outside wall was cracked into pieces small enough that he could move them a little just by stepping on them. The planned way out of the building would be to take apart one of the bunk beds, the main frame of the bed was light angle iron with a factory weld at the corners. With one corner of the bed jammed against the cement floor, the combined strength of two or three men forcing the rectangle shape out of square would break it at one of the corners. After one corner broke the rest of it would be easy to take apart. They would then have four pieces of angle iron, two about thirty inches long and the other two about six feet. To make these into the serviceable tools they needed, all they would then have to do was to remove any wire and springs still attached.

The pieces of angle iron, a chamber pot, and their hands would be all the tools they had. But it would give them all they needed to dig an escape tunnel. It would not really be a tunnel, just a pit, about two and half feet deep, dug right next to the wall at about a forty-five degree angle. The first step, of course, would be to pry out enough of the loose cement to have a workable hole. The dirt and cement would all be disposed of by spreading it under the beds.

When the pit was deemed to be deep enough, the digging would continue out and up, the hole would emerge on the outside of the wall. The last few inches of sod or turf would not be disturbed until the escape started.

The rest of the platoon would not be told of the plan, until they were locked in for the night, on the eve before the escape would take place. Dismantling the bed frame, and the excavation would begin early the next morning. If they didn't get it finished before being called to the fields, the final touches would get done when they returned. It was unlikely that anyone would look in on the place during the day, but as a precaution, one of the cots would be moved over the hole.

The next step in the plan, as Ash and Jack went over the details, would be the role each of the prisoners would be called on to play. Their thoughts went back to boot camp, and the ball games the troops engaged in during evenings of free time. One of the fellows they remembered had a terrific left arm. His name was Jimmy Darwin, usually called Jimmy D. There were very few that ever scored a hit off Jimmy D. Then there was Omar Larsen, generally called Lars, who had an equally good right arm.

There were two Afro-Americans in the group, and by coincidence they both had the same first name. There was Ray Collins who went by the nickname Raycy. The other one was Ray Peters, Peters got the nickname Raypy hung on him.

The two masterminds went over the plan many times, as well as the speech that Ash would deliver when the time came to fill the rest of them in on what was to take place. At that time they would go through a semblance of a drill. Each man would be allotted a number, and it would be the number sequence that would determine who went out first, and who followed. To ensure that order was maintained, Ash himself would be number nineteen, the last out.

A lookout at the barred window, would give the signal that indicated the dog's demise. At that point number one, armed with one of the short pieces of bed frame, was to knock out the remaining layer of sod, leaving it in the bottom of the pit as it fell. He would scramble out into the open, taking the iron weapon with him. Then reach for the hand of number two, thus making his exit a bit faster. Number two was to carry the other short piece of iron, and in turn, give number three a lift out.

Jimmy D. was number three, and would be equipped with another bit of weaponry. Jimmy and Lars would each get three rocks to carry in their pockets. The rocks would be selected and smuggled into camp by Jack. They needed to be the right size for those good arms to effectively throw, a bit bigger than a golf ball would be good. Once

Jack got these missiles inside their prison walls, he would hide them under his mattress until needed.

As they emerged out of the pit, no one was to do anything until Jack, the eighth man was out. Once out, Jack was to move to the rear right corner of the building. From here he could view both the rear, and the right hand side of the structure, both of which were out of the guards field of vision. Lars, Raycy, and Raypy, would already be out ahead of Jack, and would have taken up a position at the right front corner.

As they went through their drill, a word signal was developed. The word was Jake-Aloo. As soon as Jack took his position, at the left rear corner, numbers one and two, were to start making all the noise they could, by banging their chucks of iron together, as well as yelling at the top of their voices. Three and four would add to the melee by exercising their lungs too. The four of them were to go to the rear, go past Jack, and across the back to the left rear of the building, but not far enough to be seen by the guard. The purpose of this action was to get the attention of the guard focused on the rear.

Then Jack would yell out, "Jake," a command that was to have Lars, the right hander, step into the open and fire a rock at the guard tower breaking the glass if he could. There need only be about a second of time lapse until Lars returned to the sheltered area. With Lars back safely, Jack would then yell "Aloo," the word that would send Jimmy D. into action. Jimmy would then step into the open, and another missile would be aimed at the tower, and Jimmy slip back out of sight. As the word "Aloo" left Jack's lips, Raycy would count to three, then race for the compound that housed the trucks and other farm equipment. It would be about a hundred yard dash, but Raycy, like Raypy, was fleet of foot, one of the reasons they were picked for the job. Now the order of commands was to be reversed, Jack would again yell "Aloo," sending another rock from the arm of Jimmy D. to the tower. This time it was Raypy that was to count to three and make a dash for the machine compound.

The sergeant had another good reason for selecting the two Rays for the job of getting trucks started. They had both been convicted of car theft before entering the army. Might as well put their knowledge of hot-wiring vehicles to use, reasoned Ash. The fact that they had black skin was not a factor, though Ash had confided to Jack that their skin color would make them harder to fix in a rifle scope.

The compound had a walk-in door on one side and near the front of the building. There was a small window above the door that was nearly always left partially open. One of them was to boost the other one to the top of the door, and thus enter through the window. Once inside, the door could be opened to let the other one in. Now they would need to get two trucks running by hot-wiring them as they would have no ignition keys. For light to work by, they'd rely on the matches they'd been allowed to keep, so they could smoke. Once they had two of the heavy trucks running, one was to be driven out the doors. If they got the double doors open that is, if they weren't able to get the doors open the driver would drive right into them.

If the guard was still in the tower, which would be highly unlikely, the first truck would run right into it. Being a wooden structure, it would tumble down easily. It stood to reason that no sane person would stay in the tower, while nineteen men were after him. If he did, the rest of the prisoners, with their angle iron weapons, were to look after him. What they did to the guard was not important as long as they got his rifle.

With two trucks out and running and the guard taken care of, they would be on their way as soon as possible. The next moves would be subject to a few "ifs." If the truck used as a battering ram to get through the doors was still serviceable, they would take both trucks. If not, they would somehow all climb aboard one vehicle. Any wounded were to be loaded first. Ash wanted to set fire to the compound, before leaving, as a parting gift for the Cong, but as time was going to be an important factor, the idea of a fire might not be possible. They expected to carry it all out in no more than five minutes, that's from when man number one was on his feet, until they were on the road to Saigon.

Ash would collect as many books of matches from the men as he could, not that he was going to be sitting striking match after match to get a fire started. The idea of the matches was just to have something that would burn readily, and could be scattered over other material. The matches would make it spread faster once a fire was going. It would be too slow and too dangerous to try to get gas, and use it.

Perhaps a few of the rags that were used to wipe the oil from leaking hydraulic rams would be good. Jack new of some of them, but the fire idea would be played by ear.

Meantime the assault on the guard tower would continue, the "Jake-Aloo" commands, alternated, even after Jimmy D. and Lars ran out of ammunition. It would keep the attention of the guard away from the compound.

If it all went the way Ash had it pictured, the guard would be trying to call for help via his two-way radio, they knew he had one. But when rocks started raining in on him at speeds of up to one hundred miles an hour accompanied by broken glass, he'd be getting out of there while he could.

The first to note that the guard was leaving the tower would be one of the two stone throwers. It might be from the left rear, or the front right, but an arm wave was the signal to Jack that it was time to act. Jack would yell "Charge." All the men that were now out of the escape hole would rush the tower. The men were to spread out as much as they could, so as not to be an easy target, should the guard make it to the ground and get his gun into action before any of them reached him. The first one to hit him would do so with a flying tackle, like a defensive lineman on a football field. A piece of bedframe would then be applied, to ensure no more interference from that quarter until they were well on the road.

Jack also had another responsibility, should either of the two that were to enter the compound happen to get dropped by a chance shot from the tower, he was to send a man in his place. Under no circumstances was anyone to go to the assistance of a fallen man, but silence the rifle in the tower first.

A little guy by the name of Jose Gualda, the only Hispanic in the group, would get the job of replacing either of the Raycy, Raypy team. Jose was the ninth man out. Jack would make sure Jose raced for the compound if the need arose.

Jose, like many children born to immigrant families, had experienced a very difficult childhood. His parents had entered the States from Mexico illegally to become part of a group known as wetbacks. To survive they accepted the most menial of tasks, generally in fields producing agricultural products. It depended on the demand, but the pay was usually less than minimum wage. Jose, being the oldest of a family of nine, had been sent to work in the fields along with his father as soon as he could make any kind of a productive showing.

Even before he reached military age Jose saw the army as a way to a better life. Until they were taken prisoners, it was indeed the best life he had ever known. At last he was somebody, and treated as an equal by his fellow men.

Ash and Jack had considered making Jose one of the original pair to be sent into the compound that housed the trucks. It was his slight build that caught their attention, and led them to think how easy it would be for him to slip through the window and into the compound itself. The idea was discarded as they thought it over, realizing that Jose had never ever driven a motor vehicle, much less did he have any idea of how to hot-wire one. If Jose was called on to replace one of the original team, it would mean depending on the survivor of Ray C. or Ray P. to get it done. What if they both got shot? It couldn't happen, so it wasn't even discussed.

In the plan Jack was not to expose himself, Ash would explain the reason for this when the time came. Jack could very well be their savior, when they got to Saigon. Jack knew the layout of the city, knowledge gained as a result of his ventures with George Shipley, as they visited Saigon's dens of iniquity. He would be sent in as a scout. The brothels would be the best places to gain information as to who now had control of the city. Further to that, if for some reason they never made it to Saigon, but had to disappear into the bush somewhere, they would split into two parties, with Jack leading one of them.

As Ash lay awake at night, he rehearsed the speech to deliver, when the men would be told of the escape plan. Went over it again and yet again, he did. He would tell them that, yes, there was a chance that some of them would become casualties. He would also point out that if they didn't do something soon they were all going to die anyway. As to getting shot, he would explain to them that there are only two spots in the human body where a shot was immediately fatal, the brain and the heart, both small targets. A shot through the liver will cause internal bleeding that will bring on death within an hour. He'd remind them, though, of a number of people that had been shot through the lungs or stomach and survived. His own father had taken one through a lung during World War II.

He would go on to tell them that if any of them lost their life, they would become another statistic of a war that they never should have been involved in. He would end his speech by wishing them good luck. He'd tell them the plan was well thought out, nothing could go wrong, and "When it's over, we'll have stories to tell our grandchildren."

It was another ten days until the dark of the moon, during this time Ash and Jack Nelson went over their plans again and again. Some ideas were discarded as soon as they were conceived. Examples of these were to leave one of their number lying in ambush with the rifle taken from the guard, then to follow in Mr. Dong's Honda—nope, too high a risk. Another idea was to imbed the six-foot pieces of iron in the road, at the appropriate angle to pierce the radiator of a pursuing vehicle—too time consuming, and no guarantee of it working.

They were sure the ideas they settled on would work. Yes, they could pull it off. Somehow a short piece of insulated wire was needed to complete the death-trap for the dog. Ash acquired this one day when he had been taken by truck to an outlying carrot field. Some bags of carrots were to be loaded on the truck. When his guard wasn't looking Ash grabbed a piece of hanging wire that had broken away from a taillight it was supposed to feed. A quick jerk, and he had about three feet of wire in his hand, all he would need.

The camp authorities seemed to take a liking to Jack, so as the escape plan was worked out they would take advantage of the situation. Each night Jack would stroll around the grounds for a while, and each evening he would stop and visit with the guard in the glass tower. From his forays with George into Saigon, he had picked up a few phrases of the native dialect. He could say "it's a nice evening," and a few others. The guard, in turn, seemed to enjoy practicing his English.

About three days before the planned escape, the two masterminds of the plan, decided they had better find the source of power they were going to use to electrify the mat. On this evening, before they were locked in for the night, some work would be done on it. Jack would stroll around the grounds for awhile, stopping to talk with the guard for a few minutes, just as he'd been doing for several nights now. This time Jack held the guard's attention longer than usual. He would keep him occupied until Ash returned to the bunk building.

While the guard was distracted, Ash would try to find the power line that fed the floodlight. It had to be below the earth surface, so with nothing more than a penknife that had not been taken from him, he started digging. The only tools were his fingers and the penknife. He found the line soon enough, and as expected it was sheathed in a weather-proof sleeve. Ash cut open the covering insulation with the knife, and soon had the wire he wanted exposed. It had to be the red one. About six inches of the wire torn from the truck had already been scraped bare, and pushed inside a scrap of combat jacket. When the time came, the end would be exposed and dropped under the steel mat, thus setting the death-trap for the dog. The other end of the same wire had only about a half inch of wire bared. The wire was not the solid kind, but instead it was a number of very fine wires woven together. These fine little wires had already been twisted together making a fine point, as if to be threaded through a needle.

Ash knew, just as any electrician does, you do not mess with live wires without shutting off the power source. Having no means of controlling the power supply, he would have to be careful. He held the penknife with the only contact being his fingers on its ivory handle. If only he had wrapped the handle in cloth from a combat jacket, it might not have happened.

It was as he attempted to scrape the insulation off each side of the red wire that the knife blade made contact with the power source. The electrical current traveled through the rivets in the knife handle, through his fingers, and into the ground to complete the circuit. It was as quick as the blink of an eye and Ash was dead.

As Robert Burns once said, "The best laid plans of mice and men."

Another two minutes was all he would have needed. Just insert the penknife through the live wire, once a short bit of it was bared, then give the knife a half twist, before withdrawing it, leaving an opening to thread the extra wire into. With the extra length of wire in place he'd push it all back in the insulated covering, bending the protruding end of the extra wire as he did, thus holding it in place.

A short piece of shoelace that he intended to wrap the waterproof sheath with, before returning it to the ground, was in his pocket. There would be nothing left in sight that would attract anyone's attention except the length of wire that was to be placed under the mat, and he would cover that with leaves or other debris.

Chapter 19

Prison Camp

The following investigation uncovered more than Mr. Dong expected. The extra piece of wire, unburned because it still had not been connected to anything, was found to have come from a truck that Sergeant Ashcroft had been detailed to, just three days before. Just what Ash was trying to do was never really figured out, maybe he had thought he could fix something that would electrocute the overseer himself because sometimes Dong would stand and lean against the lamp posts when talking to the men. Jack was subjected to a great deal of questioning, but he stood his ground, denying any knowledge of a plan that the sergeant might have had. Maybe it was because Jack was recognized as a good worker that they didn't want to lose. They finally gave up on him, and Ashcroft's death went into the records as being struck by lightning.

The other finding during the investigation was a small stash of carrots under the bed of one of the prisoners. They had been warned that the penalty for stealing was harsh, so he would have to be punished. No, they didn't cut off his hand. He would have been no use in the work party with a missing hand. Long Ten Dong had a better idea. They pulled all his teeth, without an anesthetic. He wouldn't think of chewing any vegetables for awhile, at least not raw ones.

The next morning, the fellow was forced back to work in the vegetable garden, with a hoe in hand. The handle of the hoe was loose and would come out of the ferrule leaving a round wooden stick with a pointed end. He gestured to the overseer to come and see the problem. When the overseer was a step away, the prisoner lunged at him, driving the pointed end of the hoe handle into his left eye. The blow had enough force to push the eyeball aside, with the weapon lodging itself inside Dong's skull. The scream of pain uttered by Dong, all but drowned out the sound of the shot from a guard's rifle that killed the prisoner instantly. Dong was carried away on a stretcher, with the hoe handle still imbedded in his head, but fortunately unconscious. He was never heard of again.

As an example to the rest of the prisoners, the body of the man shot by the guard was hung by the neck from a post in the fence that enclosed the compound. There is remained until the body decomposed enough for the torso to fall away from the head. There were no more plans made to escape, nor did anyone ever try to steal again.

The new overseer was hard to understand, but the routine that followed was the same as it had been under Dong. Reward for a job done on time, was marijuana or vodka or sometimes both. As they became weaker and weaker, there was no doubt they would die an early death. Neither Dong nor his successor could help that could they? Death from natural causes would be written into the record.

The new overseer in his halting English was able to tell them that President Nixon had been "peached." Jack didn't know what "peached" meant, he just wished President Nixon was with him now. He wondered if the slaves of a hundred years ago must have felt much like the men in this commune did. One day followed another, and without the guiding influence of Sergeant Ash, it was a downhill slide as the men got weaker and weaker over the next two years.

◆　◆　◆

One of the fact-finding teams interviewed George Shipley before they went back to Vietnam. They had information linking him to a platoon that had disappeared. George didn't mention anything about Jack having broken legs. He was able to tell them he had witnessed his platoon being loaded into a truck at gunpoint. He told them he believed the truck was heading north.

In Vietnam the team questioned the locals but found very little information. In North Vietnam they questioned government officials. They were led to believe by some of the lower officials that there were some prisoners on a collective farm, adding also that it would be useless to try to find them. The officials told the fact-finders that the Americans were so happy under their system they would not want to return to the United States. "They have found out that a better quality of life is achieved when every one works for the common good of all, and individual greed does not enter the picture." However, the fact-finding team said they would have to get their names for the record if nothing else.

It was April 1975 when Jack Nelson and his platoon were finally found. The nineteen man platoon now numbered only sixteen. One struck by lightning, one shot as he made an attempt on the life of the overseer, and one died of natural causes. It was all there and nicely documented. They were taken to a hospital in Saigon where they were tested and found to be in very bad shape. They suffered from malnutrition, dehydration, and exhaustion. Their blood samples also indicated they were all heavy drug users.

After two weeks it was determined they were well enough to be flown back to the United States. Family members back in the States were notified as soon as they had arrived in Saigon and identification was confirmed.

Doris was so choked with emotion when she received the call from Jack that she could hardly speak, "Oh, darling, I never really gave up hope. Something kept telling me you were still alive, somewhere."

It did not take long for the media to get hold of the story that American servicemen were coming home. Within an hour, there was a TV camera crew out to interview Doris.

Questions: How do you feel about your husband coming home? Will you be going to meet him part-way? Chicago, perhaps? Are you planning a homecoming celebration? Doris didn't answer the way she felt like answering. How did the stupid clucks think she felt? With it only being an hour since she received the news she had not yet made any plans.

Doris was watching TV as the cameras zoomed in on the returning men getting off the plane in New York. Bobby, now two and a half, was sitting on her lap. "Look Bobby, there is your Daddy," Doris said. Bobby said, "Daddy." Doris thought to herself, *Is that really Jack, he looks so haggard. It will take some time to get some flesh back on those cheeks.*

Jack changed planes in Chicago, boarding a smaller plane to take him to Bismark. All the time he was in agony, and had been ever since the prison camp rescue. Those two weeks in the hospital in Saigon were sheer hell. It did not matter how he pleaded, he could not get the substance his body was screaming for. He would have given anything for a few tokes of marijuana or a shot of vodka, preferably both! He told himself he would quit using drugs and alcohol once he had been home awhile, but surely he couldn't be expected to stop cold turkey, not after what he had been through.

Chapter 20

Bismark, North Dakota

Doris, with Bobby in tow, met Jack at the airport. The meeting did not go at all as she expected. Jack did not grab Bobby and lift him up onto his shoulders saying, "So, you are the man who has been looking after Mommy while I have been away." He just said, "Hi, Bob, how's it going?" and to Doris' awkward attempt to hug and kiss him, Jack pushed her away.

When they got to the Volvo in the parking lot, Jack asked, "Where is the truck?" As they drove out of the lot, he said, "Will you stop at the Stockman's Saloon? We have to go by it anyway. I'll pick up something to celebrate my homecoming." Doris was a bit shocked at the suggestion, as prior to his going away they had never even talked about alcohol, much less thought of using it. It only took Jack a few minutes to pick up a fifth of vodka, and then they were on their way home.

Doris tried but there was not much conversation during the drive. She asked if his legs had been broken and Jack told her no. Not the response that Doris expected, such as "Why would you ask that?" Just no, so Doris did not pursue the subject. Doris realized it would take time to get back to normal and she would have to be patient.

Jack didn't wait till they were home to get the top off the vodka. The first swallow burnt its way down his throat, and started a fire in his belly. There was still time for a few more swallows before driving into their yard. By then the liquor had the effect of relaxing him, even putting him in the mood for talking a bit. Once in the house he started telling Doris how much he had missed her, how much he still loved her. "It's going to be okay now." Then adding, "We can take up right where we left off."

Doris didn't know what to make of it, how his attitude changed after a few drinks, but maybe it would be as he said. *Take up where they left off.* Maybe the vodka was just a one-time thing. After all he'd been through he probably needed something to get him started, to know what to say and how to act. He might be feeling like a stranger for a while. Jack's first priority once they arrived at the farm seemed to be to get her into the bedroom. It was ironic that their second child was born exactly nine months and fifteen minutes after they walked in the door. Doris' friend Janice thought they should get their name in the *Guinness Book of Records* for that one.

Doris was not really thrilled when she found out she was pregnant, as she knew by then that Jack had some serious problems. Jack was drunk most of the time, so she was thankful that the conception had taken place when he was sober. Hopefully, the child would be okay. Surely those few drinks of vodka consumed on the way from the airport, would not make any difference. The alcohol that day had likely entered his blood stream by the time they made love, but there would have been no time for it to reach the sperm cells that had caused her pregnancy.

Jack received two years of backpay with his army discharge. The only worthwhile thing he did with the money was to renew his driver's licence and licence the truck. Most of the money was spent on booze and, as Doris found out later, on drugs.

There was never any father-son relationship between Jack and Bobby. He never tried to play with Bobby, and he never thought to buy him a gift as other fathers often did. Bobby might as well have been nonexistent for all Jack seemed to care.

Jack never even talked about getting his old job with Goodyear back. He was far too busy feeling sorry for himself, and all the army had put him through. What he did do was to complain to the army authorities about having respiratory problems. He was given an appointment for a physical examination. It was September before he was awarded a partial disability pension, including retroactive pay to the date of his discharge.

Once again Jack had money. Through some of his drinking buddies he also got to know women. Some of them were real "down and outers." There was one in particular that would oblige any man for a bottle of wine. No one seemed to know her name, but everyone called her "Spareribs." It was through Spareribs that Jack met people in the drug trade. Doris had heard of Spareribs, but she had never seen her. Spareribs was also known as the Shady Lady. Doris wondered if that was because of her lifestyle or the color of her skin.

Doris refused to believe Jack could be involved with anyone like Spareribs. She heard Spareribs was old enough to be Jack's mother. Where was he, when he didn't come home for two or three days at a time?

In regards to Spareribs, there did not seem to be anyone that knew much about her background. On thinking about it Doris wondered if there was something in her past that could be used to get her removed from Jack's round of friends. One day she raised the subject with her friend Janice. After thinking about it for a minute, Janice came up with the idea of soliciting the help of her father.

Janice's father's name was James Roberts, he had come to America from Scotland as a young man on a teacher exchange program. He settled into the city of Minot, North Dakota, and liked it so well that he never returned to his native Scotland. Instead went on to become a professor of history at a university in Minot. He was active in sports and was soon coaching a girl's basketball team and thus the nickname Coach Bobs got hung on him, a name he was still known by, while he enjoyed his retirement years in Minot. Minot is a city some two hundred miles north of Bismark.

The following was what Coach Bobs came up with.

He found out that she was born and spent her early years on a Sioux Indian Reservation in South Dakota. When she was fourteen she was persuaded by a white man, much older than her, to leave to reserve to come and live with him in a common-law arrangement. He told her that he could get her much more than she had on the reserve. The affair lasted for about two years, and then she was chucked out to fend for herself. All she left with was the few clothes she had and a baby about six weeks old. There was nothing on record to indicate what became of the child, but Spareribs herself was taken in by a Baptist minister and his wife. This was to be her home for the next two years. The minister and wife encouraged her to go back to school. She did fairly well in school, and it was their hope that she could obtain a teacher's certificate, then go back to the reservation as a school teacher. There was nothing on record to indicate if this came about or not. Nothing more was found out about her until she took up residence in Bismark, some ten years before, nor was anything uncovered to indicate how she became reduced to the derelict level that was now her mode of life. There seemed to be nothing to indicate how the nickname Spareribs came about, unless it was taken from a comic strip that was popular in that era. Spareribs was the name of the main character in the strip, a forlorn looking hound dog with the same name as the strip title. Coach Bobs, through some research had also found out that her real name was Anne Starcloud.

After Doris took a look at the information about Spareribs she decided to drop the idea of trying to get her out of their lives. The information could bring on feelings of sympathy, rather than cries of protest.

Doris tried to talk to Jack about his behavior but Jack always said, "If you know what I've been through . . ." then he would tell her that he needed time away to think.

She suggested on several occasions that they finish the renovations to the house, by putting gyprock on the ceiling. She would stress the point of the great heat loss through the V joint that was now there. "Yes, he would get it done as soon as he could, but right now he was under too much stress." The response was the same if she tried to talk to him about testing for water at the site where they had planned to one day build a new home. Shouldn't he be doing something about getting the ground ready to plant trees as he had once suggested, but it was all to no avail.

When she asked why he couldn't at least make the gate sign that they had made plans for, the response was no better. First he would have to get a piece of well seasoned fir lumber, and of course he didn't remember those "Norski" words.

Doris said, "Well, I do and will write them out for you." Jack just said, "I'll do it as soon as I get around to it, I'll need a couple of good paint brushes, as well as some good outdoor paint." Doris told him that she had bought three brushes, in sizes one inch to three inches, when she had painted the walls while he was away. She said, "I cleaned them well when I finished so there is no need to buy brushes."

It didn't make any difference, Jack never got any closer to making the sign than he did to testing for water.

How patient was Doris going to have to be? How long was this rehabilitation going to take? In August she bought him a set of golf clubs for his birthday. Maybe if he made some new friends playing golf he would forget his drinking pals.

She didn't care if he ever got a paying job. If he would just stay home and get off the booze and drugs. Doris began to notice needle tracks on his arm, so she knew he was into hard drugs. If he would only use his time doing a bit of work around the house or yard, or if he would just take up a hobby, make something. He used to be good with his hands. This was all wishful thinking. Things did not get any better. A month after she had given him the golf clubs he sold them for half of what they cost.

Doris wondered if there was any point in talking to a psychiatrist. She thought she would probably never get Jack to agree to go to one anyway. She did, however, talk to a minister at a Lutheran Church in Bismark. The pastor agreed to come and have a talk with Jack.

After a few pleasantries, the pastor went on to tell Jack that it was the Devil's demons that had a hold on his life. If he would pray with him and ask Jesus Christ to come into his life, and into his heart, he would be able to shake off these demons and get back to a normal, healthy existence. "You must realize, Jack, that with the Devil's demons in charge you will come to a dreadful end." Jack listened for a while, then said, "Look, preacher fella. Don't try to tell me about where I am going, and if this Savior actually existed He would have stopped the horror of Vietnam. Don't try to scare me with stories of going to Hell, because I have already been there. Go away and save somebody else."

Chapter 21

Bismark, North Dakota

On February 2, 1976, Doris felt labor pains coming on. Of course Jack wasn't home, so she got Janice to drive her to the hospital. Janice also kept Bobby with her. A healthy baby girl arrived later that afternoon. Doris named her Diana, after Lady Diana Spencer, a young girl that had made news headlines very often during the last few months. Lady Di, as she was called, was expected to become the wife of Prince Charles, heir to the British throne. The second name of the new baby would be Doris' maiden name. Thus the new addition to the family was named Diana Aimes Nelson, but came to be known as Di, the same as her namesake.

Not only was it nine months from the time of Jack's arrival home from Nam until the birth of their daughter, something of a record, but it was exactly three years and ten months since his entry into boot camp. On the second day of each month, Doris made a note in a diary, as she kept a record of what she did on that day, the monthly anniversary of Jack being taken from her.

Doris hoped that Jack would become a loving father now that he had a beautiful daughter. She remembered what a loving parent her own father had been, calling her princess until she was seven or eight years old. But it was not to be with Jack. As time went on he was becoming abusive toward her.

Doris tried without success to get Jack to join Alcoholics Anonymous, a group of people with the same problem as Jack. For the most part these groups were headed by people that had experienced the problem of alcohol abuse themselves, but had overcome their weakness and were now dedicated to helping others. They made the best counselors, as they knew exactly what the problem drinker was going through. Jack wouldn't listen to her, instead he'd insist he didn't have a problem. Doris decided she would go to one of these AA meetings herself. Maybe she would meet someone that in some way could help Jack without him even knowing what was going on.

She was quite impressed with the chairman's opening remarks as he said, "I am an alcoholic," and later as different ones had something to contribute, their opening remarks were always those words. As the chairman went on to tell them, "Those are the four hardest words to say, but to handle our problem, we have to admit that we have one." He told them that there is no such thing as a "recovered alcoholic." Alcoholism is a disease, and anyone afflicted with it has to live with it, "One day at a time." He told them that every night as he went to bed, he said to himself, "That's one more day of abstention" and those one days had now added up to seven years, four months, and five days. Doris was impressed, but how could she ever get Jack to go that route? How to get him to say, "I am an alcoholic," she didn't know.

Then one day Doris read of a newly formed group called Alanon, they were the families of alcoholics that had to live with the problem drinker. Doris noted there was such a group right here in Bismark and they were holding a meeting the following Wednesday evening. Doris decided to attend, as she could not see where she had anything to lose. The first thing she found out was that she was not alone. It reminded her of the meeting of the Wives of the M.I.A. that she had attended. The subject matter was, of course, different, also the age of those in attendance. These people ranged in age from seniors right down to children of no more than ten years. While the ones attending the Wives of M.I.A. meetings, Doris remembered, had all been about the same age. She was surprised to find out how many there were in the same situation as her.

She thought the guest speaker outlined the attitude of the problem drinker perfectly. Alcoholics, he said, will always feel sorry for themselves, they will blame others for their situation. They want to lash out and hurt someone, usually those closest to them. They will say mean things to the very people that want to help them. As Doris listened, she thought, *Sir, you are describing my husband to a tee.*

When little Di was six weeks old, Jack decided it was time to resume sexual activities. *Heaven forbid,* Doris thought, not only was she afraid of picking up some disease from him, but she did not want to chance another pregnancy either. She needn't have worried about the latter, because Jack was now impotent, likely from drug and alcohol abuse. He blamed Doris for his inability to perform, he told her he could find better stuff than her in the back alleys of Saigon.

When Doris started to cry, Jack just got up and got dressed. When Doris asked where he was going, Jack told her, he was going somewhere where he wouldn't have to listen to her blubbering.

Doris came to the conclusion that Jack was not going to get any better. She was worried what kind of a life the children would have living with Jack. She finally decided that for the good of the children, she would have to leave Jack. She had talked to her sister Laura in Dayton, Ohio, about her situation. Laura was sure Doris could find a position in a dental clinic in Dayton.

Doris felt that Jack's days were numbered, given the lifestyle he had chosen. No! She did not wish him dead, but she knew it would be inevitable. She had to decide whether to stick by him until the end, or salvage something of her own life by leaving.

Doris had even gone to a psychiatrist, "Bring Jack in for treatment and we will see what we can do," Dr. Anoppollis had urged. "His dependence on alcohol and drugs is a means of hiding from his past experiences, but this has only made matters worse." When Doris suggested to Jack that he make an appointment with the doctor, Jack told her she was probably having an affair with the "shrink." "That's what he keeps a couch in the room for," he said.

To plan to do it, to move out that is, was one thing, but bringing herself actually to make the move was another. One voice said, *For the sake of the children, get out*; another told her it was her duty as a wife to stay with him till the end, "till death to us part" the vows had said. *Till death to us part*, mused Doris, *Isn't the man I exchanged vows with dead already. Surely the vows didn't indicate that I must live with this stranger that has possessed Jack's body.*

So it went during that terrible summer of '76 and into the winter of '77. She came to accept Jack as he was. The suggestion he see a psychiatrist, that had only ended in an argument, was about the last effort Doris made at trying to get Jack to change his ways.

Even when he was home there was very little to talk about. She discouraged further sexual advances by telling him to go and find his back-alley Saigon stuff. When he was home Doris slept on the couch, and never took her clothes off. It reminded her of when they first moved into their new home and she had never slept because of the mice. This arrangement lasted until Diana was a year old. The final decision to make the break came as a result of a letter from her sister Laura, telling her of a job opening in a Dayton clinic, where the dental assistant was going on maternity leave.

With her mind made up, she prayed to God for His forgiveness, as she had taken all she could. She made arrangements to move to Dayton.

It was a Monday morning in February, Jack had not been home for a couple of days. Doris thought he was probably shacked up at Spareribs' place again. She left him a note:

> I am leaving with the children so they can have a chance at a normal life. Growing up in a single parent home may not be the best, but it will be better than what we have.
>
> I will say it one more time, try and get your life together. I know you had a bad time in Vietnam, but there are others who have had the same experiences, and they have been able to get on with their lives. You have to do it for yourself, no one can do it for you.
>
> Remember how good we thought our life was going to be? Remember how happy we were when we finally got Bluebell's first calf to drink from a pail? You do remember that, don't you? His name was Argus.
>
> Goodbye, Jack. I wish I could say I love you.
>
> Doris

Doris packed their clothes and loaded the car, leaving barely enough room for her and the children. Diana, of course, was sitting in her car seat. Bobby, at four and a half years, wondered why he couldn't take his chickens with him. "No, dear," Doris said, "the chickens wouldn't understand and would be very upset about leaving their home." He was consoled somewhat when his mother said they could take Ginger, their pet cat, if he held her on his lap.

The chickens came about when Doris bought twenty-five one-day old chicks about a month before Jack came home. The hatchery had put in an extra one. They had good luck with the chicks and they all survived. Bobby was fascinated with the little balls of fluff as they ran about. Bobby made it his chore to look after the chickens, or at least he thought he was doing it when he went with Doris to feed and water them. After the chicks feathered out, they found out they had thirteen pullets and thirteen roosters. In the fall when the pullets started to lay, Bobbie was busy gathering eggs. He thought it was funny when the roosters would crow and he tried to mimic them.

Doris found out from a client at the clinic how to sever the heads, pluck, draw, and cut up the birds for the frying pan. Once the roosters were big enough she started killing one every once in awhile. The killing had to be done while Bobby was in daycare or asleep. Doris remembered how she, herself, had felt about killing mice. It would only be natural for Bobby to get upset about killing chickens. *My, how I've hardened in the last two years,* thought Doris. Yes, it was hard to kill that first one, but a quick blow to the bird's neck, as she laid it over a chopping block, with a hatchet in hand, and the job was done. Each time after that, as she saw how a chicken with its head cut off acted, it became easier.

Doris was quite pleased with her efforts. Jack had even complimented her on the fried chicken. He had said, "Old Colonel Sanders has nothing on you." In October, Doris killed and dressed the rest of the roosters, and put them in the deep freeze.

◆ ◆ ◆

When Jack read Doris' note, he shrugged and said, "What! Happy! Who would be happy about a stupid calf drinking out of a pail. If this Almighty, they all believed in, had wanted calves to drink from a pail He would have put their nostrils up above their eyes someplace, so they wouldn't drown when they stuck their nose in the pail."

122

Chapter 22

Bismark, North Dakota

So Doris was gone, *Well, who needed her?* Jack reasoned. Maybe he would have Spareribs move in with him. In a way it would be fun living with Spareribs. She must have read a lot when she was young, as she knew about a lot of places. Sometimes they would make up a game pretending they were traveling. One would make up a line about where they were going to go, then, the other one would make up the next line. They had been to all sorts of places; chased leprechauns in Ireland, ridden a camel train across the Sahara, and gone skiing in the Swiss Alps. Jack guessed it was silly, but it was fun while they were sharing a joint. Spareribs never nagged him about getting his life back together, she just accepted him as he was. She was not like Doris.

After thinking it over he decided against having Spareribs move in as he realized that a little of Spareribs went a long way. He didn't think he wanted a steady diet of her. Thinking of diets, what on earth did the old girl live on? He had never seen anything that even resembled a meal at her place. Thinking back, he thought the fare on the farm in North Vietnam was probably better than anything Spareribs served up. Decision made. He definitely was not going to ask Spareribs to move in with him.

Jack soon discovered that with Doris gone, so was her paycheque. He needed more money than his army pension provided. He thought that if he had the title to the five acres, he could sell it and make a good profit.

He thought bitterly that Doris' parents could have coughed up the whole cost of the farm instead of just giving them the one thousand dollars down payment. They had lots of money, but they didn't consider the hardship they had put on Jack and Doris by saddling them with a mortgage. Oh, Doris had kept up the mortgage payments while he was away. Big deal! It was from the allowance out of his wages. Doris must have paid off that promissory note, they had had to sign when they got the money to buy Bluebell. Jack wondered, *Perhaps her dad might have had a change of heart, after I went to Nam. Maybe the old bastard forgave the note, and did not insist on repayment. It wouldn't have hurt him any.*

Jack's thoughts turned to his old army buddy, George Shipley. He still had George's address. George had been clever with a pen, and maybe with his help they could make a legal looking document that would pass for a title that would enable him to sell the acreage. Sure, it was a bit dishonest, but hey, the country owed it to them. He wrote a letter to George.

In April, Bluebell had another calf. At this time of year one of the local ranchers often had a cow lose a newborn calf. They would pay good money for another newborn to adopt to their cow. So to raise some much needed cash, Jack took the newborn to the Auction Mart and got one hundred twenty-five dollars for it.

Had it been two weeks later, a portion of that one hundred twenty-five dollars would have been garnished. When Doris got to Dayton, she not only got a job and a place to live, she also got a court order for child support in the amount of one hundred dollars a month for each child. This was done with a certain amount of coaching from her brother-in-law, Ben. Doris thought it was a waste of time as Jack could never hold down a job. Ben explained it would come into play if Jack ever tried to sell any of their assets, the land, the livestock, the truck, or anything else. Anything, that is, that was sold through the public forum.

Jack never did receive a reply from his friend George. However, he did receive a letter from one of George's sisters informing him that George had been convicted of forgery and was now serving a one year sentence in jail.

The summer dragged on. It was probably because Jack drank a lot of milk that he stayed alive at all. Bluebell produced well, in spite of irregular milkings. He made some effort at planting vegetables, but grew more weeds than anything. Corn seemed to grow the best. When cooked up, the feed of corn on the cob reminded him of that poor guy in Nam who had his teeth pulled because he stole some vegetables. Jack couldn't remember his name, but even if they hadn't shot him, he would never have been able to eat corn on the cob again. He had more corn that he could eat, so he put some in bags and froze it.

It was awhile now since Jack had received the court order to pay two hundred dollars a month in child support. He laughed about that, as the only income he had was the miserable army pension. He didn't think they would touch that, as it wasn't enough even for him to live on. Especially not when he had to have his bourbon or a joint to help him face life. He knew he would have to get more money, just for himself to survive. He thought he might sell old Bluebell. Argus, of course, had gone to market a couple of years ago. He still had Bluebell's 1975 calf, a heifer named Daisy. They should bring a few bucks, but if he took them to auction, he would have to pay half the proceeds in child support.

What to do? How to raise some much needed cash? The thought then occurred to Jack that *Hey! His Uncle Andrew had made him a beneficiary.* He wondered if the old bugger was still alive. Not likely, anyway, that home he was in would have gone through all the money he might have had by now. Forget Uncle Andrew.

It then occurred to him that he might be able to grow a real cash crop, marijuana. He would be able to keep himself supplied plus sell some, he knew there would be a market for the stuff. He could grow it the same way they did on the farm in Nam. He wasn't going into that sophisticated hydroponics crap. He thought about where he could get his hands on a substantial amount of seed. Those cronies he used to drink with would likely know of a source, but they seemed to have melted away over the summer. Jack wondered if his lack of funds had anything to do with it.

To grow marijuana, not only would he need seed, but he would also need help. Where could he find help for an enterprise like that? Then the idea struck him, his half-brothers. Maybe he could interest them in a partnership. Gee! He could hardly remember their names, Olafson was the last name. That was the creep his "old lady" had married. Those boys, let's see, they would be about eighteen years old by now. They should be willing to help out, after all, it was largely due to Jack's efforts that they had had food on the table when they were growing up. They owed him. One was named Harold, the other mmm . . . Helmer. Yes, that was it—Harold and Helmer Olafson. He decided to contact them.

Doris had told him his mother, Sophia, had left the States to go back to Norway. This had happened while Jack was in Vietnam. It came about when her sister Helga lost her husband. Helga had never been blessed with any children, so it was only natural that she became closer to her sister Sophia, who was also finding herself very much alone then. Unlike Doris, she had accepted word of her son Jack's presumed death as fact. It was less than a year she got the news of Jack that both of the twin boys decided to strike out on their own. Harold got a job on a ranch in Montana and seemed satisfied. Helmer found employment with an extra gang on the railroad, a job that took him to various locations in the northern states. She seldom saw either of them any more, it made her feel much less wanted. There were times that word of their being in Williston reached her, but they never took the trouble to call.

When Helga had suggested they return to Norway, where they could spend their twilight years, Sophia warmed to the idea immediately. Helga had heard there were some good retirement homes in Oslo now. It sounded like just the thing. The farm that had been their childhood home was only a few miles from Oslo. As Sophia still didn't have any money, she asked Helga to tell her what they would live on in Norway. "Not a problem," said Helga, "You could raise a bit of money on your own by selling your house, and if that isn't enough, there is the money I received from Erik's insurance policy. I'm sure I have more than enough for both of us." She also went on to mention their age difference, "As I am five years older than you, the day will likely come that you will be looking after me. Besides, we are going to need the companionship of each other. No need to let your conscience bother you, you will not be a freeloader." The more they talked, the more excited they got. Sophia would have no qualms about leaving her adopted country. She didn't think fate had been very kind to her. She'd lost her first husband at a very young age, and her second husband had deserted her, leaving her destitute. The country had taken Jack from her, and now her twin boys had all but deserted her. In less than a month, they had both sold their houses.

They bought airline tickets that would get them to the land of their birth. Then they converted enough dollars to kroners for their immediate need when they arrived in Oslo. The rest of their money would be transferred from an American bank to one in Norway. It would be the first time either of them had traveled by air. There would be a bus trip to Minot, North Dakota, then a short flight to Denver. After that a direct flight right over the North Pole, with just a short stop in Fairbanks, Alaska, for fuel. They were two very excited ladies.

◆ ◆ ◆

With the decision made to locate his half-brothers Jack went to bed, but he did not feel well. He felt a cold coming on, he would have to get a bottle of bourbon to take care of it.

Chapter 23

Entering the States

After crossing the border and entering the United States, Harry started to think ahead. He knew there would have to be a stop sometime to feed and water and cattle. Laws governing the humane treatment of animals determined that, and it only made sense to keep them in good condition. The stop couldn't come soon enough for Harry.

They eventually stopped and backed up to a loading platform. No one looked inside after the last animal off-loaded. They probably counted them as they went down the chute.

When the driver and the others had disappeared, Harry climbed out of the truck. It was still dusk, but promised to be a nice day. Much better than the weather he had left behind in Moose Jaw. Harry proceeded down the road to what appeared to be a settled area. He knew he smelled bad but surprisingly his clothes were not too dirty. The galoshes looked out of place, now that there was no snow. He took them off, and stashed them in a culvert, a short distance from the stock yards. No way to know what the future held, but he might retrieve them sometime.

After walking for about twenty minutes he came to an all-night diner. All of the money he had on him was three Canadian twenty dollar bills. After Lucille's funeral he had stopped at an instant teller, and made a withdrawal from his account. He was at least thankful he had done that. No way would he use his credit cards. He would have to dispose of them.

Before placing an order in the diner, he asked if they would take Canadian money. They would. He gave them one twenty-dollar bill and he received twelve dollars and fifty cents in U.S. funds in return. That gave him two good reasons for not cashing in the other forty dollars. Cashing in sixty dollars when all he had ordered was toast and coffee would seem odd, and at the rate of exchange they gave him, he knew he had been ripped off.

While the toast and coffee was being served he went to the washroom and cleaned up the best he could. He found out he was in Bismark, North Dakota.

Throughout the night while riding with the cattle, he thought of what he should do next. He would need to acquire a new identity. If there was a natural disaster of some sort; a tornado, an earthquake, or maybe a flood, that would be the place to be. Make himself useful rescuing people, until he found someone near his own age who was beyond help. Everyone would be so busy that no one would notice anyone else. There would always be some unattended vehicle around to load the body into. Then drive to an isolated area and get rid of the remains. He would keep the wallet, if there was money in it so much the better, but the important thing would be a name and Social Security number. This was not the time of year for tornadoes, however, an earthquake somewhere would be a distinct possibility. What to do in the meantime? *Harry, you are going to have to hide.*

The sun was just showing above the horizon as he left the diner. Harry started to do a lot of thinking about his next move. Had he made a mistake in his bid to escape custody? Well, it was done now, might as well try and make the best of it. The area around Bismark was for the most part a farming community. He had noted this while still in the cattle liner, from occasional glimpses in the dusk and again now in full daylight. He reasoned there would be a better chance to hide in farm buildings than in town. He knew there were a lot of farmers that went south for the winter months, at least in Saskatchewan there were, and it would likely be the same here. If he could find a set of buildings that had already been left vacant, well just maybe. There were a number of problems to take care of. The most important one was to get rid of the handcuffs. He couldn't very well just go to a machine shop in town and say, "I wonder if I could get you to cut this thing off my wrist." A set of vacant farm buildings might have a shop with a grindstone and cutting wheel attached, or even a good hacksaw, though to use that the cuff would have to be clamped in a bench vise. Harry had never in his life ever stolen anything, but in addition to the handcuffs, there were some other problems that needed to be taken care of. One example of this was the open-toed shoes he was wearing. If he could find a pair of work boots that fit him in someone's garage, maybe no one would care if he sort of "borrowed" them.

Yes, he would leave the city and head for the farming area of North Dakota. He might find someone who would give him a job, even if the pay was only for his keep. Or there might be a snowbird family that had not yet left for a warmer climate, that might be interested in having someone look after their holdings while they were gone. He knew he could present himself well, if he needed to impress someone who would not care too much about his identity. He started walking south, and what was more, a walk would air out his clothes. The clear sky indeed indicated the promise of a nice day.

When Harry had walked south for what he estimated to be about three miles, he came to what he thought was a farm site at first, but as he got closer he realized it was a cemetery. The archway sign over the gate on the east side indicated it was the Sunset Cemetery.

The cemetery gave Harry a gem of an idea. If he was to meet people, he would need a plausible story as to why he was out in this rural area, so he developed the following narrative. He would say he had just lost his wife. *At least that part of the story would be true.* As she was buried here in the local cemetery, it made him feel closer to her to come and visit the grave where she lay. Then he would add that wanting to visit the grave might seem silly to some but it was the way he felt. His story would then go on to say he had two weeks holiday. With no money to go anywhere, he thought it would be better to be out of town, and out of the house where they had been so happy together. He needed time to think and get his life in order again. Then he would go on to say that he would be glad of a job helping someone with chores, or other jobs that needed doing. The pay need not be much, he would even work for a roof over his head and something to eat. He needed to be out in the fresh air, and be able to visit the spot where his loved one lay. So with his story formulated, he had to decide on the next direction to go. There was a crossroads at the southeast corner of the cemetery. Harry spotted a set of buildings further to the west, but none on the south or east, at least not very close.

Harry headed west. He had only gone the length of the cemetery fence, when he saw a cow jump a fence near the buildings that lay ahead. After she made her escape from the pasture that held her, she headed west in the ditch. It was only another few minutes until Harry saw a truck, coming out of the farmyard. After the occupant took time to open a gate, and get back in the truck to drive out onto the road, he headed west to overtake the misbehaving cow. Harry summed up the situation immediately, thinking, *Here is my ready-made letter of introduction.*

Chapter 24

On the Nelson Farm

Jack Nelson put in a terrible night. He was in and out of bed several times, his cold worse than ever. However, no remedy could be had until nine o'clock when the outlets in Bismark opened for business.

It wasn't even eight o'clock yet. As he looked out the window he saw Bluebell jumping the fence, breaking a post as she went. Jack knew her problem. She was in heat. If he let her go, she might go for miles in search of a mate. Maybe he should let her go and get herself impregnated the natural way. *Shit, better not, no telling the damage she may inflict on a neighbor's garden or yard. Jack, you had better get in your truck and head her off.*

Since they had owned Bluebell, they had always impregnated her by artificial means. There were several technicians in the area to provide the service. The timing of the service was, of course, important. The technician had told them the ideal time was twelve hours after the heat cycle was noticed. So this evening was the time.

Bluebell must have cycled on a regular basis all summer, but with Jack being away so much this was the only time he had noticed. He knew he wouldn't do anything about it because the technician would charge twenty-five dollars. Money he didn't have, and if he had had it, he needed more bourbon. Jack was suffering worse than Bluebell. It was his association with Spareribs that had switched him from vodka to bourbon.

Doris had always taken care to see that Bluebell reproduced on an annual basis until now. She had learned of artificial insemination through reading what books she could on the cattle industry. It would not have made sense to keep a herd sire for one cow. *Yeah, good old Doris was always reading something.*

As Jack got in his truck to go after Bluebell, he remembered a letter he had received from Doris when he was in boot camp. Doris had watched the procedure of artificial insemination, and her letter had explained in detail the steps taken by the technician. Then she had added the sly footnote, wondering if Bluebell had enjoyed it. Jack didn't know what made him think of that now, but he remembered smiling when he read the footnote.

In spite of Bluebell's urgent need to be on her way to somewhere, she did take time to take a few bites of the lush green grass in the ditch, the only grass that was still green. This gave Jack time to open a second gate back into the acreage, as he knew he couldn't get her to jump back where she had made her escape.

After a few bites of grass, the cow continued westward in the ditch. With the truck it was easy enough to get ahead of her, but Jack had to get out of the truck, and into the ditch on foot to turn her back east again. Had he tried, he probably would have been able to just walk to her, take hold of her neck strap, and lead her back to the corral. Jack was in no shape to take on anything that strenuous. Just getting in and out of the truck taxed him to the limit. *How did I ever manage to lead her those three miles, on the day that we bought her?* thought Jack. *What has happened to me, to get so weak . . . Well, once I get over this cold.*

After waving his arms and yelling he got her moving again, this time back in the direction she had just come from. He turned the truck around, with the idea that if he kept broadside of her to the open gate, he would use his legs again to chase her through it. Bluebell didn't cooperate, before she got far enough to be opposite the gate, she decided the lush green grass was too good to pass up. When she stopped for more grazing, Jack tried to get her moving by blowing the horn on the truck, but Bluebell paid no attention to his efforts. Jack got out of the truck and tried throwing a few pebbles at her. This got her going again okay, but before Jack could get back in the truck, Bluebell came up out of the ditch to cross the road to the north side.

From west of the cemetery fence and continuing on for the next half mile or so was a cornfield, while nearly ripe, it had not been harvested. Jack could see that if Bluebell made her way out of the ditch and into the cornfield, there would be no chance of stopping her. At the same time he saw someone on foot just west of the cemetery and was about to call to whoever it was and ask for help. However, at this point Harry, who was still pretty agile and was close enough to act, had the situation well in hand.

As Bluebell came out of the south ditch to cross the road, she was obliging enough to stumble a bit while making her way into the north ditch. This gave Harry the extra time needed to make a run for it and be able to grab the neck strap the cow wore. Once caught she was docile enough. Harry was easily able to lead her back onto the road. When Jack drove up beside Harry and Bluebell, he got out of the truck saying, "Well, mister, you came along just in time." He then introduced himself as Jack Nelson. Harry shook his hand saying, "Blair Simpson here." The name Harry chose was not a spur of the moment thing, as he walked, he had decided that he needed a name to introduce himself by. There was no particular reason for the one he picked, unless he thought the initials B.S. being the same as Bud Soelen would make it easier to remember.

Jack went on to tell Harry how under the weather he had been feeling, and said he "must have picked up the flu bug and now this damn cow won't stay in." It was than that Harry went into his story of bereavement, with the two weeks vacation, and no money to go anywhere. He emphasized a bit about the proximity of the cemetery, and his desire to be out in the fresh air. Then he added in his offer to work for nothing.

Jack thought this over for a minute before he said, "Well, Blair, we just might be able to help each other out. I need some help. My old lady ran off with that nigger baseball player awhile back. Got my place in a bit of a mess, and I just can't seem to shake this flu bug and keep up with my chores." *My*, thought Harry, *a racist remark like that in Canada could land you in a peck of trouble. There must be laws against racism in this country too. I think the black people are generally referred to as Afro-Americans*, but he didn't comment. Jack went on to say he only had a five acre farm and a miserable pittance of a pension from the army for his stint in the Vietnam War.

Harry told Jack he would be glad to help out for room and board as this would give him a couple of weeks of fresh air and time away from the stress of city life and the memories of his wife. "Well, if it's just fresh air you want, there is plenty of that here," replied Jack.

134

Jack told Harry he would need to go into Bismark in another hour or so. He never explained why, but said he would go back to bed for awhile because he had hardly slept last night, and the chase after Bluebell had really knocked him for a loop.

"In the meantime, Blair, if you like to make yourself useful, you could get what milk you can out of Bluebell, but it won't be much." He mentioned Bluebell's current problem. "There should be a couple of posts behind the shed, maybe you could replace the old that damn cow broke off."

Harry went looking the place over while Jack went back to bed. It occurred to Harry that this was just what he was looking for. He noticed empty bottles at the back of the house, and decided this guy was a loner and would need help. Maybe he would pose as a long-lost brother, so anyone that noticed there were two of them would not pay any attention to a stranger in the country. Harry would wait until they were better acquainted before putting this plan into action.

Jack was also doing some thinking. There was something wrong with the story Blair had handed him, if Blair was his real name. For one thing, who would be walking four miles from town? Didn't he have a car, and walking in those shoes? Those open-toed things were not much more than bedroom slippers. Harry, as we remember, had stuffed the galoshes in a culvert. The cap he was wearing said "Moose Jaw Sportsmen's Center." Wasn't Moose Jaw somewhere in Canada? Yes, it was. Jack remembered fixing a tire on a truck once that had a Canadian licence. The driver had said he was from a place called Moose Jaw. Jack remembered thinking at the time, *What an odd name for a town.* Blair's story didn't add up. This might be the kind of help he would need in his marijuana project. Not only did he need some-one to do the work, but also he needed someone to take the rap should they ever be caught.

Jack did not go back to bed right away, instead he watched Harry's activities. When Harry went into the back shed, Jack heard him turn on the grindstone with the attached cutting wheel. *Now what was he up to?* When Jack went to peek through a crack in the shed, he saw Harry take off his coat and make short work of the handcuff still attached to his wrist.

Now Jack did go back to bed. He would not say anything about the handcuff right now, but if this guy tired to be difficult about the marijuana scheme, Jack would have a lever to use. They would have a heart to heart talk when he was feeling better.

As Jack lay there, and thought things over, it occurred to him that it would take at least a year before there would be any revenue from the marijuana project. So what to do for income in the meantime? Well, if this Blair fellow had a job as he said, his wages would likely be enough to get by on. *Come off it, Jack, the guy has escaped from somewhere and has no more of a job than you have. Maybe he could get a job though, hmm, doing what? Hey! Suppose he was to pose as me and get the old job back with Goodyear Tire, it's five years now.* The personnel will have changed enough that no one would notice that Jack Nelson was a different person, and anyway people do change. But as Jack thought on it a bit more, he came up with a better plan yet. He would apply for his old job back in person. He would likely get it, as veterans were generally given a preference. Then with the two-way phone, he would be working from home as he did before Vietnam. Except that this time when the repair calls came in, it would be this Blair fellow that would go out to do the work. Jack might even go out on a couple of calls just to get him started. When it came time to pick up the paycheque, it would be Jack that was on hand to do that. The more he mulled the idea over the better it seemed, as it would give him complete control over the finances, letting him use the money as he wanted to. With these encouraging thoughts dancing through his head, Jack fell into a deep sleep.

While Jack was formulating the plans that would determine his future, Harry went about the tasks that Jack had suggested with a renewed sense of security, once the handcuffs were removed. The thoughts going through Harry's mind were not much different than the idea Jack had hit upon. Instead of being a brother, why not become Jack Nelson in person, and with his identity get a job. Of course, Nelson would get the paycheque, but at least there would be some money to survive. Yes, in a day or two they would talk about it.

He found a pair of old rubber boots that fit him fairly well. They would be better than what he had been wearing.

Jack was right when he told him, he would not get much milk from Bluebell. About a quart was all he was able to squeeze out of her. He knew he would have to repair the fence before letting Blue-bell out of the corral. He found the replacement post where Jack said he would. With the post over his shoulder, a crowbar, a hammer, a hand-operated post-hole auger and the handcuffs in his hand he headed for the hole in the fence. He used the bar to dig out the stump of the broken post. He used the post-hole digger to make the hole about six inches deeper than it had originally been.

After dropping the handcuffs in the hole and covering them with enough dirt to bring the hole back to its original depth, the new post was put in place and dirt packed around it. If the post was ever re-placed again, the handcuffs would not be found. Harry was glad to see the last of them. After the wire was stapled to the new post, the job was done.

He turned Bluebell out on the grass. There was a heifer, that ap-peared to be about a year old, out there already. *Likely Bluebell's calf from last year,* thought Harry.

Harry then saw what looked to be some kind of effort to grow a garden. It was overgrown with weeds, now dead and long since gone to seed. Mixed in with the weeds were a few dried up corn stalks and not much else.

The shed, while having nothing that would match the equipment the workshop on the farm of his friend Jake Myers contained, did nonetheless boast a reasonable assortment of tools. Harry decided that his fellow, Jack, must have taken some pride in his work at one time. After finding a garden rake, he went about the job of piling the weeds and other debris in the center of the garden. Then he put a match to it. Once it was burning well, he added his credit cards, driver's licence, and all other identification to the fire. He even threw in his Moose Jaw cap. Damn! He wondered if he had been wearing that at the diner. Well, maybe nobody paid any attention to it. There were likely lots of people from Moose Jaw who stopped in there. Once the garden was cleaned up, he returned to the house. Jack was right again. The house was a mess. It reminded him of Lucille's ef-forts at housekeeping.

Jack was still asleep, he was breathing in gasps and seemed to be in a cold sweat. Harry found another blanket and covered him. What-ever he had to do in Bismark would have to wait.

Harry managed to get a couple hours of shut-eye himself, waking up when he heard Jack stirring. When he looked in on Jack, he was struggling to get the covers off. It looked like he didn't even have the strength to do it himself. Harry suggested that he try to see a doctor. If he wasn't up to driving, was there a neighbor who could help out? Harry never offered to do any of the driving himself. However, Jack thought he would be all right if he could just get a little more rest. He told Harry nobody cared about him anyway.

No one to care about him would be understandable, it will be remembered that before Nam the newlyweds were trying to get so much done that they had never met any of their neighbors. They had never given Sam, the fellow at that auction, another thought.

And after Nam? Well, the people he associated with were not exactly the type to rush to his assistance in an emergency. Jack said he hadn't eaten yet today, "Blair, maybe you could find something in the deep freeze to cook up for us to eat." A search of the deep freeze left Harry wondering what on earth this guy lived on. The only thing that even resembled meat was part of a roast chicken that should go into the garbage, probably something left from when the runaway wife was still around.

Again the stories told by his father about the Depression years went through Harry's mind. Old Frank often spoke of the wonderful stews his mother, Harry's grandmother, could make out of a jackrabbit. Harry remembered seeing a rabbit burrowed in along the cemetery fence, but had thought no more of it when Bluebell caught his attention. He wondered if it was still there.

He had already noticed a twenty-two caliber rifle in the shed, probably used to kill gophers in the garden. He went out to the shed to get it and on looking in a wall cupboard he found a part of a box of shells. Harry knew that because it was getting late in the day and a rabbit being a nocturnal animal, it would likely take off at the first sign of danger, since it would soon be out foraging for food. That morning he must have been within fifty feet of it as he passed by on the road, but there was not much chance of getting that close now. With the loaded rifle in hand, he would see what he could do.

He made his way towards the cemetery, but stayed inside the fence, and on Jack's property. It would mean shooting across the road. He hoped there would be no traffic. He was still about a hundred yards away when he saw that the rabbit was still there, but the rabbit saw him too. It picked up its head, raised up on its front legs, and was ready to go. There was no time to do anything but put the gun to his shoulder and fire. It may have been a good shot or just a lucky one, but the rabbit leapt about four feet in the air, then came down and kicked a few strokes before lying still.

It turned out to be a nice fat buck with very little meat destroyed by the shot, just part of one shoulder. He took it back to the shed to skin and dress it out, then cut the carcass into pieces. Not having done this before he was quite surprised at the amount of meat there was, the hind quarters and loins were very good.

He then put the meat in a frying pan to brown it a bit before it went into a pot that was going to be stew. While the meat was browning, he again made a search of the shed where a few withered turnips were found. While raking the garden he had uncovered some small potatoes. Thus he had the ingredients for a stew, a part bottle of ketchup, found in the fridge, was added, so the result was quite a palatable dish. There was also a half a loaf of bread in the fridge. A hearty meal called supper was ready at about half past four on Tuesday afternoon.

Jack was pleased to see supper on the table when he got up, but he didn't eat much as he was feeling worse. He did drink some of the broth from the stew and said it was good. Later that evening he developed a high fever, so Harry helped him back to bed.

Harry then looked around the bathroom and found Jack's razor and had a shave. He left his sideburns on. He thought that if they were left to grow for awhile it would change his appearance. He would try and pick up a pair of horn-rimmed glasses. He needed to change his appearance as much as possible, now that he was a fugitive from the law. After the shave and a good wash he lay down on the couch again.

It was starting to get dark, when he noticed Bluebell at the corral gate. He knew she probably needed to be milked again. The yield was again about a quart of milk. The morning's milk was well chilled in the fridge, so if Jack woke again he would try to give him some milk. Harry wondered if Jack was used to anything as mild as milk.

Harry did not rest much as he was up most of the night, applying cool damp cloths to Jack's forehead in an effort to reduce his fever.

Most of Wednesday, Jack was delirious. Most of his muttering could not be recognized as anything. He did come through fairly clear once in awhile, and Harry heard him say, "Doris, guess what, honey, I got Argus to drink by himself." Harry didn't know what he was talking about, but thought Doris might be the runaway wife. Later he said, "I fixed a tire for a trucker today, and he told me he had lots of raspberries at home. He told me he would dig up some roots and bring them to us the next time he came through. Just think, honey, if we plant them this spring, we should have berries next summer." Still later, more muttering, "Do you think Mistress ever settled back to her normal lifestyle with the cat lady?"

Harry had heard the term "death rattle," and the sounds Jack was now making could well be described as a rattle. He couldn't just remember, but thought it was handed down from the days of the sailing ships. Sailors stricken with scurvy, high fevers, or other ailments made a rattling sound as a result of labored breathing. This was supposed to indicate that death was imminent, and it usually was. He remembered reading sailing stories of how sharks would follow a vessel that had someone aboard with the "death rattle." Stories that left the reader believing that somehow the sharks knew that a hearty meal would soon be tossed overboard for them. *Maybe they did,* thought Harry, some animals seemed to possess a sixth sense that made them aware of situations that we humans miss.

Anyway whether it was the "death rattle" prediction or not, at about six o'clock that night, Jack Nelson died. *Now what do I do? Harry asked himself. A voice inside his head said, Harry, don't be a fool, fate has sent you an opportunity, take this guy's identity. Fate already gave you the storm, the accident, the train, the cattle liner, the cow in the ditch. Don't go soft now.* Harry thought it over. He remembered Jack saying that nobody cared about him, so it would seem he did not have any family or friends.

140

Chapter 25

The Bismark Acreage

Survival was instinctive, this was the opportunity Harry was waiting for, a new identity. He thought over the plan he had developed while riding in the cattle liner. Find a dead body, take the identity, and leave the remains in some isolated spot. The more he thought, the more holes he found in the idea. A human corpse gets found. It gets identified. Then where would he be if he was caught posing as Jack Nelson, with Nelson already proven dead. As there were no sharks about to feed him to, there had to be another way found to dispose of the remains.

That cemetery at the corner just a little to the east, no one would ever find or even think to look for a dead body in a cemetery. There would be an ideal place to deposit Jack's remains. He would need an open grave, and for that he would have to find a funeral notice somehow. The TV probably had one of those channels that carried funeral announcement as well as other coming events. He turned on the TV and switched to the community channel. After about ten minutes there was an announcement of a funeral on Friday afternoon at three o'clock.

The deceased had at one time been mayor of Bismark. That would be good. The dear mayor would help draw a crowd for Jack's departure.

The funeral would be the day after next. Someone would likely open the grave the next afternoon. With this decision made, he found some light nylon rope, the same rope that had tied down the insulation batts when Jack first went shopping for material to renovate the old house. He used the rope to tie Jack's feet together, and also to tie the arms to the side of his torso. He sure didn't want his limbs spread-eagled when rigor mortis set in. He then covered the body with a sheet. With this done, Harry went to bed.

On Thursday morning after milking the cow, Harry looked into another small outbuilding which was a bit off from the others. He had already noticed a few hens around it. On opening the door, he could see that Jack had not given the place much attention. It would need a good cleaning as soon as possible. The nests needed to be lined with straw, or maybe grass. He found over two dozen eggs that were not broken. He knew some of them were likely stale, but he would break them into a dish before putting them into a frying pan. It looked like it would be eggs for breakfast and milk to drink, as he had not found any coffee.

After breakfast, he started considering how to keep vigilance on the cemetery without being too conspicuous. Walking? *Better not, some passing motorist might stop to offer me a ride, and whether I accepted it or not, the incident might be remembered.* He knew he was lucky this hadn't happened on his walk out from Bismark. The truck would also be a no-no. He had destroyed his Saskatchewan driver's licence, but wouldn't have used it anyway. He had found a current driver's licence in Jack's wallet, but Harry didn't think the photo of Jack resembled himself enough to fool a traffic officer, so he wouldn't try using it.

Harry didn't give the matter much thought, but when Jack had returned from Vietnam, he had renewed both the truck and driver's licence, so they were both good for five years. If renewal had been on an annual basis, as it was in Saskatchewan, Jack likely would have let them both lapse by now.

So, Harry, what are you going to do? He remembered seeing a bicycle in the shed. It was leaning against the wall, behind some bags of insulation batts. A bike would be the answer. When he got it out where he could take a look at it, he could see that the bike was in good shape except for flat tires. It was obvious it had not been used for a very long time. Harry couldn't know it, but the last one to ride it had been Jack's Uncle Andrew.

He found a hand tire-pump. However the leathers in the plunger were dried out so badly that the pump would not work, not even when he smeared oil on the leathers with the dipstick from the truck.

The hose on the pump, with an adapter to attach it to a valve stem, still looked good, so he hit on what he thought was a novel idea. The spare tire on the truck was well inflated. Harry got a screwdriver and loosened the clamp holding the hose to the pump. Then he screwed the adapter to the valve stem of a bike tire. The cap on the valve stem of the truck tire had a forked end for tightening and loosening the Shrader valve. Once the valve was loosened and the air from the tire escaping, Harry slipped the open end of the pump hose over the truck valve stem and tightened the clamp. Presto! In a matter of seconds the bike tire was inflated. He did the same with the other tire. He now had a serviceable means of transportation.

Harry was proud of his accomplishment and wondered if the magazine *Popular Mechanics* had ever heard of fixing bike tires that way. Harry took the bike for a spin and it worked well. When he checked later he found the tires still held air.

When he rode past the cemetery about three o'clock, he saw the backhoe opening a grave and a truck nearby with a rough box in the back. At the intersection, instead of going past the cemetery gates he turned south until he found another intersection, where he turned west. He continued on, turning north to reach the road back to Jack's buildings. He could check on the cemetery again when it got dark. Also, it would be good to become more familiar with the area.

When he checked again that evening everything was in place. The rough box was in the grave. The backhoe was parked beside a small building near the west side of the cemetery. Harry was sure he could operate the backhoe. It was the same make as one of the contractors had used when natural gas was brought to Tudor. That was when Harry had two weeks holidays and had spent his time off working for the contractor.

Now to move the body to the grave site. He would have to chance using the truck. He would not turn on the headlights, it was a clear night, the light from the night sky would have to do.

With the truck backed to the door, he rolled poor old Jack, (yes, at twenty-eight he was already an old man) onto a blanket on the floor. He then dragged him to the open end gate of the half ton. The body was stiff now. It would almost stand on its own, *More than he could do when he was alive*, thought Harry.

When Jack had gone back to bed after watching Harry remove the handcuffs, he had only removed his outer clothing. With the corpse dressed only in underclothes it just didn't seem right to send him into that cold ground without a covering of some kind. With the body now in the back of the truck, Harry decided he should pull the blanket edges up around him, then pin them together like a shroud. For pins he went to one of the trees for a few twigs about the size of pencils. Once stripped of bark and whittled to a point, he had dowel pins that easily pierced the blanket, and thus kept it secure. Harry couldn't know it, but the blanket was the same one that Jack and Doris had covered old Andrew's bed with for that first night in their new home. Yes, the one that was a wedding present.

So with Jack Nelson in the back, Harry left the farm yard shortly after ten at night. He drove to the cemetery, and parked as far from the road as possible. He climbed on the backhoe, started it, and got down to the business at hand.

The chains and hooks for lifting and lowering the rough box were in the bucket. Harry had just got the bucket lowered over the rough box and was about to get out of the cab to affix the hooks to the rough box when he saw the headlights of a car coming from the east. *Careful, Harry, it's likely just someone going by*. The car slowed down as it approached the intersection and turned north, Harry was glad he had had the presence of mind to shut off the backhoe motor. The vehicle's headlights swept the cemetery as it turned. Harry flattened himself to the ground on the far side of the backhoe bucket. How much had the occupants of the car seen? Well, at least the bucket on the backhoe was down. When the car came to a stop outside the cemetery gates, Harry could see the dome light of a police car. His heart was really in his mouth. *Should I try to hide among the gravestones, or go over the fence and try to make a run for it?* Would he need to do another disappearing act? How much evidence of his presence, had he left at Jack's house? He couldn't remember. *Should I try to pass myself off as an employee who had stopped to make some repairs to the rough box, telling the cops it had been damaged when they unloaded it?* No, not likely they would swallow a story like that at this time of night.

Two policemen got out of the car. He could hear them talking and it was not about anything out of place in the cemetery. One said he had noticed an advertisement in their branch office that the White House was looking for security people to provide protection for the former president, Richard Nixon. He thought he might apply, it would pay better than this crummy job. The other fellow replied, "Well, I guess old Tricky Dickey is going to need all the protection he can get. I suppose the job would be okay if no one shot you." Harry could hear another sound too, and realized the officers had just stopped to relieve themselves. They were not nearly as relieved as Harry was when they into their car and drove away.

Harry continued with the job he had started, and fitted the grab hooks into the rings on the rough box. By the light of the stars he lifted out the rough box and set it beside the grave, then scooped out one large bucketful of earth. He was about to spread it over the pile of fresh dirt that was already there. He changed his mind, as it occurred to him that a bucket of extra dirt would likely be noticed when the grave was being closed. *Do not take any chances, Harry,* so he just lowered the bucket to the ground, with the earth still in it. After the body was removed from the back of the truck, he could dump the dirt into the truck box to take back to the farm, where he would spread it out in the chicken house. The chickens would like that, especially if he could find some clean straw to spread over the dirt.

Right now the next move was back to the truck for poor departed Jack. Once the truck was backed up to the grave, he just rolled the remains to their final resting place. In the dim light of the stars he was not sure, but he thought the body landed prone and face down in the fresh excavation. *Bury him seven feet deep and face down, so he won't come back,* was the well worn metaphor that crossed Harry's mind. It was a term one person might use in an effort to degrade someone else. Though as the phrase came to him, Harry felt quite sure that Jack wouldn't want to come back, even if he could, not to the quality of life he'd been experiencing.

Then he lowered the rough box back into the grave with the back-hoe bucket. Harry was pleased with his efforts as the box went right to the level it had originally occupied.

He returned to the house, parked the truck and went to bed, in Jack's bed. He would wash the sheets tomorrow. It had been a trying day, but it was behind him. Tomorrow would be another day.

Harry didn't really intend to show up at the funeral but, *Gee*, it didn't seem right to send poor Jack off without some kind of a farewell. He would not go to the church, but would attend the grave-side service.

Harry while not enamored of any particular religious philosophy, didn't think that he fit the role of an atheist either. Oh, he believed in everlasting life all right. Anything that could reproduce itself would have everlasting life, through succeeding generations. Further to that, the memories of the departed that lingered in the minds of those left behind could be considered as life everlasting. He also believed there would be no more pain and suffering after death, and he believed in a place called "Hell." It existed right here on earth. Some of it was being visited upon him right now, in that he was having to withdraw from all he knew and loved.

Still, as he reflected on his own situation, he could think of all sorts of people who were worse off than he was through no fault of their own. At least he still had his health, and considered himself lucky in that respect.

If this wonderful life beyond the grave really existed, why wouldn't everyone be eager to get there, rather than hang on by a thread to a life that had no quality whatsoever, he mused. *Why does a human have to be forced to endure months or years of agony, while a dog in the same situation can be put down, and suffer no more? I guess with mankind being able to do such unthinkable things to their fellow man*, Harry reflected, *if euthanasia were used it would be abused.*

He biked to the cemetery, arriving slightly ahead of the funeral procession and blended in with the crowd. As the minister was offering prayers, Harry closed his eyes with the following thoughts, *Heavenly Father, I ask you to take my friend Jack unto You and forgive him any trespasses he may have made against his fellow man. Please erase from his memory all the sorrowful experiences endured during his time on earth, especially those times in Vietnam. Please lead him safely through the gates of eternity, so that he may know peace and tranquillity forever, and Jack, if you can hear my thoughts, I thank you for your name and identity. I shall try to never do anything that would disgrace your name. Lord hear my prayers. Amen.*

Harry felt better as he left the cemetery and returned to the farm.

That evening as he summed up his situation, the following thoughts came to him,

Well! Harry, old boy, it's been quite a week. You've been to two, no, make that three funerals, been arrested for murder, escaped custody, ridden a freight train, ridden with a load of cattle as fellow travelers, entered a foreign country to become one of their citizens without reporting to immigration officials, and taken a new identity. So what lies ahead?

Chapter 26

The Bismark Acreage

Saturday morning and time to take stock. The first thing Harry had to do was learn all he could about his new identity. The shoe-boxes of papers and junk revealed very little, but a battered old suitcase in a closet contained Jack Nelson's army discharge papers and birth certificate.

Harry would now be known as John Ingvald Nelson, born in Williston, North Dakota, on the fourteenth day of August, 1949. Social Security number 532-741-002. The number was on the army discharge papers and would be needed to get a job or transact any business deals.

Harry would go under the first name of John, there would be less chance of anyone who knew Jack making the connection. He must also remember that a Social Security number was not called a Social Insurance number, the identification system used in Canada. *Canada. Will I ever see Canada again?*

He could not find a title to the five acres of land, but if it was mortgaged, a bank would hold the title. He did find the farewell letter that Doris had written when she pulled out. On reading it he understood something of Jack's rambling about Argus, when he was delirious. It also came to him that Doris had had good reason for leaving and there was no other man involved.

Harry, now called John, had only changed his age by a couple of months with the new identity. He was still twenty-eight years old. The few clothes found in the closet did not amount to much but fit not too badly. They were certainly more serviceable than the clothes he was wearing when he left the cattle truck. He had already made use of one of the shirts and a pair of shoes to wear to the funeral. He also found about ten dollars in change and dollar bills in the house. This brought his total cash on hand to just over twenty dollars and he still had the forty dollars in Canadian funds. He needed groceries but he knew he would have to be frugal.

Saturday afternoon he rode the bike into Bismark. He would try to find a job, anything would do.

A Payless Shoe store had a "sales clerk wanted" ad in their window. He tried there, but the manager was not in, he was asked to come back on Monday morning. At Safeway's, he bought two loaves of bread, a pound of coffee, a pound of margarine, a jar of Cheese Whiz, cereal, two onions, two pounds of hamburger, and a box of laundry soap. Enough food to supplement the milk and egg diet somewhat. Perhaps he could get another rabbit to add to the list. Though he'd had enough stew for awhile, as the rest of Wednesday's supper had been his fare for the following two days. The bill for the groceries was fourteen dollars and ten cents. Harry then biked back to the farm.

Harry spent all day Sunday, scrubbing the floors and cleaning the house as best he could. He also cleaned out the chicken house. He noted there was not one bit of feed around for either the cattle or the chickens. With winter coming on, it would be a must to obtain feed, but how, with his limited resources? If he tried to sell something, it might attract too much attention. Well, he would think about it for awhile. At least they were all right for now. If he could just get a job.

On Monday morning Harry, alias John, was at the door of Payless Shoes when they opened for business. He knew it was a job he could handle as he had plenty of experience working with the public. He walked into the store and presented himself well to the manager, who hired him on a trial basis. The wages were not good, but they were better than nothing.

Harry rode the bike back and forth, for the four mile commute to work. The reasons for not using the truck were obvious and with his limited funds he could not afford gas. *Besides*, he thought optimistically, *this was a good way to improve his physical fitness.*

Things went smoothly for the next month. Harry had an outgoing personality, so sales increased at the shoe store. Customers were soon telling their friends how obliging the new clerk was at Payless. The manager even complimented him. Harry received his first paycheque, netting three hundred forty one dollars for two weeks work.

Harry had also managed to exchange the remaining forty dollars of Canadian money. One day while his co-worker had gone to lunch he rang up a "no sale" on the till and took out the right amount of U.S. funds at the rate of exchange listed for that day. This was common practice, as it often happened that someone from Canada would make a purchase with their own currency. Then when the receipts went to the bank at the end of the day, the exchange was made back. The customer was usually short-changed a bit, but Harry didn't care. He needed U.S. currency.

The two week paycheque arrived just in time, because the next day there were two pieces of mail. One was from the power company telling him he was in default of payment, and service would be discontinued if the current payment, together with arrears and penalty for late payment were not made by October 31. It totaled one hundred ten dollars. Harry paid it.

The other was a form letter from the Department of Defense, advising John Nelson he would be required to have a physical examination by November 1, in order to bring his records up to date. Failure to comply would result in his pension being discontinued. Harry, posing as John, did not appear for the physical.

For the most part, the job at Payless was routine, one day followed another, but on occasion something happened to break the monotony. One such time occurred while Harry was looking after the shop himself. He noted a woman, probably in her thirties, coming through the door. Her arms were laden with a number of shoe boxes. It turned out there were five in all. Harry thought she was going to return all of these for a refund. *Gee, I wonder if there is even enough money in the till to handle the transaction.*

As it turned out, the boxes did not contain shoes. Each box had about two inches of dried clay in the bottom. In the clay of each box was the imprint of a child's right foot. Each box was marked with a name; Michael, Helen, Walter, and so on. She wanted Harry to fit each child with a pair of shoes, using the imprints for size. She said she would select the style and color.

Then she went into a long narrative as to the disposition of each child. There could be no duplication of shoes. You see, Mike would get really upset if he had to wear shoes that were the same as Walter's. She said she would have brought the children with her, but they could be a bit of a handful for one person to manage. "They are so ambitious and inquisitive, but then I guess it is only natural for children of their ages, which range from nine down to three. Why, just last week I took them with me grocery shopping at the A & P, and would you believe it, they got some boxes of rice off the shelf and before anyone noticed they were busy throwing handfuls of rice at each other. All except little three-year-old Barbara, that is, she couldn't get a box open, so she thew a whole bottle of ketchup. The bottle was glass, so it broke and did make a bit of a mess. I thought ketchup was all in plastic bottles now, with child-proof lids, but I guess not. Anyway, the way the manager ushered us out, you would have thought we were a gang of terrorists, for heavens sake. The kids likely got the idea of throwing rice from that TV commercial advertising Uncle Ben's long grain rice, where you see that movie star Betty White throwing the stuff. Oh, but how I do ramble on. Do you think you can get the right size of shoes using these prints?"

Harry told her to come back after lunch, when he would have the shoes all packaged up and ready to go. He thought to himself, *Well, I'm glad you never brought the little darlings with you. I will see what I can do with their sweet little footprints.*

He had a good scare one day, however, a day that he didn't bring his usual bag lunch, so was having lunch in the restaurant next door. On these rare occasions he always sat so he could see out of the front window. It was a quick exit to the washroom when a car pulled up in front and the person getting out was a former fellow worker from the bank in Moose Jaw. He watched from the bathroom, and was ready to duck out the back door, but was more than relieved when the guy bought a pack of cigarettes and went out again.

As the weather got colder, Harry had to decide what to do; not only about the livestock, but how would he continue to get to work when the snow came? There had been a couple of mornings already when there had been a slight skiff that melted off by noon. He couldn't see himself selling shoes for the rest of his life, so maybe he should

151

try to get something else, something that might pay a bit better, but what? When the weather got bad should he try and get an apartment in Bismark? Rent would take a big bite out of his paycheque. What to do about the cattle and chickens? Maybe try to find someone to keep them over the winter with their own herd, but that would take money. Try and sell them, that might be the best solution.

His questions were partly answered for him, when the manager called him into his office as the second month began, saying, "We really like your work, John, but you haven't told us everything about your background. I have a court order to garnishee 50 percent of your wages. You are in default in child support payments to Doris Kathleen Nelson in the matter of support for your two children, Robert Hunter Nelson and Diane Aimes Nelson."

Harry was struck dumb. It took him awhile but he finally managed to tell the manager that he hadn't made any payments because his wife had left him for another man. "As a matter of fact, I have a lawyer working on it right now, trying to get the court order struck down," he said in defense.

The manager said, "This may be all very well, but I have no alternative but to obey the court order and turn the paycheque you have coming over to the court. You can keep the one that arrived two weeks ago, since you are allowed to keep half your pay. There is one more thing, nothing personal you understand, but it's company policy. We cannot keep you on the staff. Payless feels anyone in your position may be a risk. I am sorry, but I have no control over it. Good luck to you, John, and if you are able to get the court order struck down, don't hesitate to come back and see us."

Chapter 27

Bismark, North Dakota; Dayton, Ohio

Harry spent the weekend lying around the farm. He knew if he went somewhere for a job, the same thing would happen. He found a picture of Jack, with a woman who must have been Doris. She was stunning. He already knew from the court order that she now lived in Dayton, Ohio.

He thought about Irma. Should he try to contact her via the code system they had worked out? She would no doubt come to him if she could. At least she knew he had never killed Lucille. If she did come, it would only make the situation worse. It would be harder for the two of them to stay hidden. Besides, the police were likely watching her every move. They would have clued into his connection with Irma from his friend Jake Meyer.

Perhaps the best thing to do would be to go home and give himself up, and then face trial. Irma would surely testify that he had been with her on that fatal afternoon but would they believe her? Testimony would reveal that they both wanted to get rid of Lucille. Lawyers had a knack of badgering a nervous witness with a series of the same questions, asked in a different way, until they got the witness to contradict themselves. Why Irma might even be charged as being an accomplice to murder. *No Harry, you had better forget about Irma for now.*

He thought of the unjust twists the "path of fate" had taken as he went down the road of life. If only he were able to undo that incident in the back seat of a car in Tudor, Saskatchewan, so long ago. How long ago? It seemed a lifetime, and because of it he had lost out on a university education, and was now a fugitive from the law. *Lucille Harper, damn your soul to the fires of Hell. Careful Harry, perhaps she didn't have a soul.*

Many thoughts went through his head, perhaps re-enlist in the army, now that he was using Jack's identity. Maybe get posted to a foreign country somewhere, and then just disappear. No, for one thing a medical exam would prove him an imposter. Anyway, what would he do in another country, he might as well have gone to jail.

The more he thought about it, the idea of going to see Doris seemed to be the best alternative. He could manufacture some story about how he had the same name as her ex-husband and by a computer error had the same Social Security number. Harry was smart enough to realize the computer was on its way to becoming part of everyone's life. Though so far they were still a new invention that many people had only heard about. The business sector was about the only place they were being used, and he knew from the bank that mistakes did get made, and once made it took an expert to correct them. Yes! If he handled it right, this woman Doris might just accept the computer error story, and lift the court order that garnished half his wages. She must realize she would never get anything out of Jack anyway. He would be cautious about giving her too much information, but could tell her he had met Jack because of the Social Security number error.

There were a few problems to take care of first. The cattle and the chickens could not be left unattended with no feed and winter approaching. Money was the other problem. No reason why these two problems couldn't take care of each other. He would run an ad on the same TV channel that he had seen the funeral announcement on. It would not attract the attention the Auction Mart would. Those auctioneers wanted you to give them a whole lot of information regarding the item for sale. There would be no phone number on the ad. Harry had already found out that the phone was dead. Service discontinued due to lack of payment, no doubt. If he ever tried to get phone service in the name of John or Jack Nelson, the outstanding account would have to be paid. Well, that was a bridge he would cross when he came to it. He decided to have any replies to the ad forwarded to Jack's post office box number in Bismark, North Dakota.

Another thing to do was go to the company that supplied electrical power, and have them discontinue service. This would prevent the account going into arrears, with penalties tacked on again.

As a result of the ad, he sold the truck, the two head of cattle, and the ten chickens. He thought of trying to sell some of the tools and the bicycle, but the less contact with other people, the less attention he would create. As he had no way of knowing what the future held, it might be better to hang onto the bike. A different matter with the truck, because if he could sell it, it should bring a substantial amount of cash. The cattle and chickens needed to be sold for humane reasons. The chickens only brought fifty cents each. A Chinese restaurant thirty miles south of Bismark bought them. It was good they were able to pick them up. Harry guessed they would end up as chicken balls in Chinese cuisine. The truck, with the low mileage, brought a good price and he did not do too badly on the cattle.

In total he raised one thousand seven hundred and fifty dollars. He didn't feel guilty when he considered he had given Jack quite a bit of help, not only doing a few chores, but he'd made Jack's final hours as easy as he could. It was Harry that had come as close as he could to giving Jack a Christian burial. Had Harry not been on hand, Jack's remains might have just stayed where he drew his last breath. How long might it have been before someone looked in on him? His body would have been terribly decomposed and difficult to identify. To add to it all, there was the matter of the lost wages from Payless Shoes. *No! There was no need to have a bothered conscience over the one thousand seven hundred and fifty dollars.*

When Harry had been going through Jack's papers he had never found anything to indicate that there was a bank account anywhere. It was unlikely he would have used it anyway. He was glad now that he had opened an account when he got that first paycheque from Payless Shoes. He had paid the power bill by cheque.

Now with the money from the truck and cattle in the form of cheques, he deposited them into his account using the Automated Teller Machine, then withdrew four hundred dollars, which was the limit the machine would allow in one day. He could always get more money as he needed it, at a branch in some other town.

Harry spent most of the four hundred dollars on some new clothes, a suitcase, and a bus ticket to Dayton, Ohio. As soon as he arrived in Dayton, he rented an inexpensive motel room.

Now to meet Doris. He knew he would not be able to knock on

her door and say, "Hi, honey, I'm here to take up our life again."
Even if he had looked like Jack, he'd need a better approach than that
to meet the person called Doris.

He found her house and watched it for a couple of days. He noted
that a young girl arrived at the house every morning around seven-
thirty. Likely a babysitter, as Doris left the house shortly after and
board bus number eighteen. On the third day Harry also boarded bus
number eighteen just before it got to the stop where Doris would be
getting on.

When Doris boarded the bus Harry was quick to notice that she
was even prettier than her photo indicated. She was wearing a uniform which looked like a nurses' uniform. He thought she probably
worked in a clinic. When Doris got off the bus, Harry got off the bus,
and followed her as she entered a mall and went down one of the
wings. He noted that she opened the door to a dental clinic with a set
of keys from her bag.

Harry then went for coffee to think things over. He did have a
tooth that needed attention. So he finished his coffee and went to the
dental clinic to see if he could book an appointment. Doris handed
him a form to fill out and told him there was a cancellation at nine-
thirty and if he wished to take that appointment he could.

When Doris noticed the name John Nelson on the form she ex-
claimed, "That is my ex-husband's name."

Harry then asked if she had ever lived outside Bismark.

"Yes, but . . ."

"Do you have two children named Robert and Diane."

Before Doris could respond another customer came in, the conversation ended.

Doris thought about their strange conversation during the rest of
the morning until coffee break. If this was some kind of scheme of
Jack's, he could just forget it. If this was another George Shipley, he
could get lost. This guy seemed different, he was at least polite, and
she was curious about what had happened to Jack. So when Harry's
dental work was complete, and he asked if she would like to join him
for coffee on her break, Doris accepted.

Over coffee Harry explained to Doris that he had met her former
husband, and how as a result of a computer error, they had the same

Social Security number. He told her how his wages had been garnished at the shoe store and how he had lost his job, but he did not tell her that she was now a widow. Well, legally she wasn't since no death certificate had been made out for the departed Jack Nelson. *No use going into all of that.*

He repeated the story Jack had told him of her running off with another man, leaving out the "N" word. "Lies, all lies," Doris said. All she left with were her two children, a few personal items, and her old car. She told him something of what life had been like with Jack after Vietnam.

Doris looked at her watch saying she had to go back to work but it would be nice to continue the conversation later. "If the weather is still good next Sunday, I could make a picnic lunch and we could meet in the park across the street from where I live. You may like to meet my kids, being as you have helped to support them."

Harry replied, "I would like that." She gave him her address, as well as that of the park. *As if Harry did not already know.*

The picnic in the park went well even though it was late November, it was like a midsummer day. Harry had had the foresight to bring gifts for the children. Little Di, now almost two years old, got a mechanical calf. It was covered with hide and hair that resembled a real calf. It was battery operated and when turned on it would walk ahead a few steps, then stretch its jaw forward and utter a few plaintive calls just like a calf in search of its mother. Then it would repeat the procedure by walking some more. Di, on her chubby little legs, would run after it, clapping and yelling. She wanted to cuddle it and rub her face in its fur.

Even Bobby, now almost five years old, was intrigued with it, but he was more impressed with his own gift. A bat and ball, the bat being the right size for a boy his age. Harry spent some time pitching the ball to Bobby, who was really thrilled if he hit the ball. Of course Harry would actually try to hit the bat with his pitch.

The lunch was enjoyed by all, after which they played on the swings, climbed a ladder to a slide, although Di had to be lifted up, and they crawled through a series of painted tires. By three o'clock the children were tired and ready for a nap.

Doris told him it was the best day the children had ever known.

They had never received gifts from their father and he had never taken time to play with them. Doris asked Harry, alias John, if he would like to come over to the house and have supper with them. "Yes," Harry said, "I would like that very much."

That supper was only the beginning. On the following Tuesday Harry called again with a flyer in his hand. McDonald's was running an ad, with two hamburgers for the price of one. Would Doris and the children like to go? Being old enough to understand what the conversation was about, Bobby answered before his mother could. "Oh boy! McDonald's. Can I have french fries and a coke?" That being settled, they were off to McDonald's for supper. Neither of the children did much with their hamburgers, but were sure excited when they could play on the slides and swings that were in the room set up especially for kids. Harry had brought a Polaroid camera, and with Bobby sitting beside Ronald McDonald the clown, took his picture. When Bobby saw the picture he couldn't get to Doris quick enough, so he could show it to her. Doris could see by now that her children were absolutely fascinated with this new man that had come into their lives. In short, they idolized him.

In that same week something happened that put yet another turn in the pathway of Harry's life. The father of Doris' babysitter got a promotion and a transfer that meant the family would move to California. Harry offered to look after her children until she could find a replacement for the sitter. Doris saw this as a satisfactory solution for the while. There would be no need to worry, the kids were more content with the man she had come to call John than they had been with her teenage sitter. Bobby, of course, went to kindergarten, but only for a half a day, he was always home by noon.

On the following Monday, Harry was there about a half an hour before Doris went to work. It didn't take much instruction on where to find whatever he might need, what to get for lunch, and so on. Then she gave him the office phone number and was off to work. When she got home not only was supper ready for the children, but for herself as well. Once she had her coat off, Harry told her he hoped she'd find everything okay, and he'd be back in the morning. "Oh! but surely you'll stay for supper won't you?" Harry stayed for supper. During supper Bobby told his mother about the games that Uncle John had played with them. Blind Man's Bluff, Pin the Tail on the Donkey, and more.

It was the next evening when Bobby said, "Why does Uncle John have to go home, he could sleep in my bed, and I can take the top bunk," that changed the arrangements yet again. Doris looked at the man they now called Uncle John, and said, "You know, you've never told me where it is you are staying. With friends here in Dayton perhaps."

When Harry replied that, "Well, no. My home is a nearby Super Six Motel," Doris said, "Well, why spend money on a motel? You're welcome to take Bobby up on his offer and save the motel bill." Harry was more than glad to hear these words because if he kept spending the way he was he would soon be broke.

They were all happy with the arrangement, little Di still slept in a crib in her mother's room, so every night Bobby would have his Uncle John all to himself. Harry read him a story every night, and could make all the associated sounds, as the Billy Goats Gruff trip-tropped over the bridge, or in Jack and the Beanstalk the Fee Fie Foe Fum was just like the giant did it. The same thing with Goldilocks and the Three Bears, and so on, Bobby was simply fascinated.

What followed about a week or so later was almost sure to happen when two young adults of the opposite sex share close proximity. It was one night after the children were in bed, Harry was drying dishes as Doris washed them. Doris put her hand on the side of his face saying, "Have you always worn sideburns? They really look good but you should have them trimmed, and your moustache could do with a bit of a trim too, I can do it for you if you'd like." Harry pulled her toward him and kissed her, she melted into his arms. The intimacy aroused in Harry a desire that comes natural to the male of any species, so it was to Doris' bed they went, without even finishing the dishes.

When the dishes were finally done and it was time to go to bed, this time to sleep, Doris wondered if he wanted to move to her room on a permanent basis. Harry said, "There would need to be something wrong with me not to want that, but for tonight I should go back to Bobby's room. If he woke up in the night and I wasn't there it might upset him, but if you explain to him tomorrow that the sleeping arrangements are going to be changed, he will likely accept it."

As Doris had some holiday time coming, she phoned the clinic and got the next day off. As Di was too young to understand, Doris waited till Bobby came home at noon, to explain the changes to be made. She started out by saying, "You really like Uncle John, don't you?"

"Oh, yes," said Bobby, "He tells me lots of stories."

"But you know he's not really your uncle, don't you?"

"Well, yes, I guess so."

"How would you feel about it if he were your daddy?" said Doris.

"You mean be my real daddy?" said Bobby.

Doris meekly replied, "Yes, he would like to be your real daddy."

"Oh boy, that's neat, I'll tell the kids at school. They always told me I didn't have a daddy."

"How will you go about explaining why he hasn't been with us all the time?" added his mother.

"I will say he had a job that he couldn't leave, but he's here now and he's going to take me fishing. Arthur said his daddy couldn't be here because he was working."

Doris knew about Arthur's dad. Rumors had it that he had been in a mental institution. She secretly hoped there would be no rumors like that about her man, John. She merely said to Bobby, "Don't you think a story like that would be lying?"

Bobby said, "I wouldn't be lying, Mommy. He did promise to take me fishing."

Doris thought, *You little rascal, you've got the makings of a politician, must be a trait handed down from your great-grandfather.* Then she went on to tell Bobby that they would be changing the sleeping arrangements. His sister was really getting too big for the crib, so she would sleep in his room on the bottom bunk. Your new daddy will sleep with me, because daddies and mommies always sleep together. Bobby wanted to know if his daddy would still read him stories, and Doris was sure he would.

To Harry the situation went beyond the wildest dreams he might have envisioned on that long ago morning, when he vacated the cattle liner and started his trek into the farming community of North Dakota. It was a mere two months, but to Harry it seemed long ago. His thoughts that morning had not gone beyond getting a job for his room and keep.

Chapter 28

Dayton, Ohio, One Year Later

It wasn't long after settling in as part of the family that Harry got a job in a local bank. This came about largely as a result of the influence of the husband of Bobby's kindergarten teacher, Emile Anderson.

Emile had been impressed with Harry the evening that the Nelson's had invited them to their home for an evening of playing bridge. While they were having coffee, Harry got Emile on the subject of his job at the bank. Harry said he had some experience in the banking business himself, without elaborating as to where he had gained his experience. He indicated he would like to give it another try. Emile told him there just might be a chance, as the bank where he worked would be advertising next week for a junior clerk. Harry applied for the job, and was naturally nervous as to how an interview might go. How much would he need to reveal of his past? He was pleased they didn't ask for a written résumé. *What on earth could I have put in one? Heavens! If they searched the school records of the real Jack Nelson, it would be revealed that he couldn't even do simple arithmetic, much less handle the columns of figures the banking industry would expose him to.* The one-on-one oral interview went well. The questions for the most part dealt only with banking. Some hypothetical situations were put before him, and he was asked to explain how he would handle them. The interview resulted in him being hired on probation for a period of six months. When the six months probation was over, if he met the bank's expectations he would become a permanent employee. He took to the job like a duck to water, and eventually rose to the position of Loans Manager.

There were two situations brought about as a result of taking Jack's identity. One was the telephone, and as Harry expected there was an outstanding account along with a late payment penalty. Harry paid it in full and converted the same number that Doris used to their joint names, John and Doris Nelson.

He worried as he approached the other problem, thinking it might not be as easy to handle as the telephone had been. He would need an Ohio driver's licence in the name of the departed Jack Nelson. It would be a real test as to whether his cover would work or not. If the Traffic Bureau would accept the story he had planned for them, he would become a citizen of the United States, with proper proof that he was indeed John Ingvald Nelson. However, if his story didn't stand up to the scrutiny it might undergo, he could be exposed as an imposter. While he really was, he didn't like thinking of himself that way.

He had some nervous moments that morning at the Traffic Bureau as he gave the name John Nelson, along with the Social Security number and produced Jack's army discharge papers and birth certificate for identification. He informed the clerk he had just moved here from Bismark, and in moving had lost his North Dakota licence. He asked how to go about getting an Ohio licence. The clerk keyed the information into the computer. Jack's name came up on the screen and as it showed no traffic violations, the clerk told him she could issue a licence right away. "Since your licence in North Dakota is current you don't have to take a road test, John," the clerk advised, "I will just take your picture for your Ohio licence, collect the registration fee, and you will be all set." She also made the comment that, "it was time you had a new picture anyway." The one that appeared on the screen as she brought up the North Dakota licence must have been taken a long time ago." It doesn't look much like you do now. I guess it's because you have a moustache now, that makes you look so different, besides you weren't wearing glasses before," she commented. As she went about taking his picture and completing the document, she chattered away all the time. Harry had prepared himself to some extent for the dialogue that followed. He was pleased as he answered her questions, as to why the move to Dayton, do you think you'll like it here, have you ever been here before, and so on.

It was her comment made as she handed him the driver's licence that really shook him. She looked at the discharge papers and said, "Oh! You've been in Vietnam, my brother was over there too."

Oh! Oh! thought Harry, *Is she going to ask me for names of places I've been?* She did ask him how long he'd been there, and Harry said, "Oh! about two years."

Then she said, "My brother thinks getting involved with that mess was the stupidest thing this country ever did. What did you think of it?" As Harry was trying to respond with some degree of intelligence, two more people walked in wanting the clerk for something. Harry thanked his lucky stars for the interruption that ended the chitchat, and walked out quite pleased about it all.

As he made his way home, he made a mental note that he would have to bone up on Vietnam. Maybe with minor changes he could use some of his Dad's war stories. Yes! He would be ready in case he was questioned again about his army service.

◆　◆　◆

They kept the old Volvo that Doris had brought with her from Bismark. The previous year they had acquired a Ford Aerostar Sport van. This was the ideal vehicle for their little family, as it had lots of room behind the seats to carry stuff when they took the children on outings.

Before he started work at the bank, he raised the subject with Doris regarding lifting the court order to garnishee part of his wages. Whether Doris accepted the computer error version or not, Harry couldn't be sure, but she readily agreed to have it done and sought the help of her brother-in-law Ben in doing so. Once Harry was assured that his job at the bank was permanent, they opened a joint account, and just like any other average American family both of their paycheques went into it.

As Harry reflected that things could be worse, he thought of his miserable life with Lucille. He felt lucky now to come home to an orderly household. Meals were always on time and Doris excelled in the art of culinary cuisine. The children loved Harry and called him Daddy. Just last week little Di came bursting in the door from kindergarten, saying, "Daddy, Daddy, I got first in my class for painting!"

Harry looked at the colored picture she had, and told her she had done very well. She had stayed inside the outlines of the characters, even if her choice of colors left something to be desired. He didn't think she would ever find a purple horse, but he kept that thought to himself.

They had enrolled Di in dancing lessons. There were several different age groups all looking very beautiful in their costumes. Di was in the preschool group and they were dressed as bumble bees. The auditorium was packed with proud parents and it was the preschool class that stole the show. Not because they were that good, but because of the funny mistakes they made.

The Nelsons had now developed an interesting social life. They exchanged card-playing visits with friends, sometimes they went dancing, other times they would go and watch Bobby play ball. He was in Little League.

However, both Doris and the new man in her life were harboring feelings of unease. Doris knew there was something in his past that he was not telling her. When she attempted to get more information about his meeting with Jack, he was so evasive. She had already told Harry about Jack's addictions. When she asked if, on meeting Jack, had he acted as a normal person might, the reply was, "Well, he was quite thin and pale looking." She asked about the appearance of the inside of the house, "Well, he hadn't been in the house, as Jack was out in the yard when he was there."

Other than on that first encounter during coffee break, they had never really talked about the computer error that had given Harry the same Social Security number as Jack. Doris wanted to believe his story, and gave a lot of thought to the possibility of it being true. The dental clinic she was employed at had one of the things, a COCS 286 it was called, and she knew from experience that if the wrong information was keyed in, it was hard to correct. Doris actually hated the thing, with its box of paper with perforated margins that made the paper feed up through the printer, then the margins had to be removed, and the sheets of paper separated. It was used to keep a record of each client's dental service, to print out bills, and to keep a record of payments. Doris always felt she could do it faster by hand.

However as time went on, the clinic upgraded to a computer called a 450. It was much easier to operate. The print-out sheets were not joined together, but came out individually on a tray. As to making mistakes, it did happen, but Doris could correct them herself, just by touching the delete key, then typing the correct information. No! The story of the computer error was too far-fetched to be true.

Could he have somehow met Jack and, wanting to escape some part of his past, done away with him, so he could take Jack's identity? No! She did not believe the man she called John could commit murder. But he might have found Jack dead, disposed of the remains somehow and gone on from there. This seemed to be more likely, but she could not pursue the matter. Life as she knew it now was good. She would not chance losing it by asking too many prying questions.

Harry also did a lot of thinking. Should he tell Doris the full story of his past? He was sure she would believe him if he explained that, while he did not know who killed Lucille, one thing that was certain, he had not. Yes, he felt that if Doris knew all the facts she would keep his secret with him. On several occasions Harry almost told it all. The chance of being recognized was becoming more remote, as more time went by and a full moustache and sideburns adorned his features. But the off chance was always there, someone from back home might see, and still be able to identify him. What would happen if such a situation came about, and it was established that Doris knew the full story. Why, she could be charged with harboring a fugitive from justice. No way would he see her having to bear a burden like that. No! Life was good, it was best to leave well enough alone. That was the way their relationship would continue. Whatever it was that went unspoken between them could remain that way.

A good example of the lie they were living, had to do with the acreage at Bismark. They would liked to have just sold it, but to do that they would need some assurance that the real Jack Nelson would never show up. During that first winter together on raising the subject of the acreage, Doris said the payment anniversary of the mortgage was January third of each year. It was now February and it was unlikely that Jack had made a payment. Doris told Harry how she had kept up the payments while Jack was away. She had built up a good equity, and would hate to lose it as a result of default. They decided to make a trip to Bismark on the coming weekend if the weather was nice, and it was.

A number of reasons were set out for the trip. The first consideration would be to take care of the overdue mortgage payment, plus any extra interest resulting from late payment. Then they would try and find some trace of Jack, both of them knowing, of course, that no trace would be found. Until proof of Jack's death was established, they decided the best thing to do would be to try and rent it out. It gave Doris a sort of morbid feeling when she realized this was the second time she had been looking for proof of Jack's demise. On arriving in Bismark on Friday afternoon the first thing they did was call at the bank that held the mortgage, and as expected the last payment was in default. Once that was looked after they took a motel room for the night, neither of them suggested going out to the acreage. They then agreed that Harry (known as John) would search the old haunts that Jack had frequented, as Doris remembered them. He would stop at the farm, after all Jack might have died and still be in the house. As it was unlikely anyone would look in on him, this was a possibility. While Harry was doing all this, Doris scanned the ads in a local newspaper to see if there may be anybody interested in renting property such as they had.

Harry went about trying to find someone that might know what had become of the missing Jack just as if he expected to meet him face to face. He called on the notable Spareribs, she couldn't remember the last time she had seen Jack. She thought Harry was kind of nice and suggested she could make it worth his while, if he would like to spend some time with her. Harry didn't have the time. He then made a few calls to the bars Doris had suggested he might try. Very few remembered Jack at all and those that did, couldn't remember when they had last seen him.

He did actually stop at the farm, and found it much as he had left it in early November. The real purpose of the call at the farm was to enable him to tell Doris at least something that wasn't a lie. So when he got back to the motel he was able to tell her there was no indication that the place had been occupied in some time. He had not seen any cattle or chickens about, nor had he seen any sign of a truck. The only comment Doris had to this was, "Maybe he disposed of the cattle, and has left the country with the truck."

Meantime, Doris had found an ad that looked promising. A phone call put them in touch with a man that had some rodeo horses and was looking for a spot were they could be left when they were not on the circuit. He did not want the buildings. This rounded out the situation perfectly. If Jack ever came back, the buildings would be available. The rental money would take care of the taxes and future mortgage payments.

Another thing for Doris to face was what to do about her parents. She couldn't have them meet her new man without some explanation about what had happened to the old one. They wondered why Jack hadn't come with her on the couple of occasions she had gone back to Williston with the children. He was always too busy. She would tell them that, yes, Jack had a few problems after his stint in Nam, but except for a slight respiratory problem, he was fine now. He wasn't able to go back to Goodyear, as handling those heavy tires would have been too much for him. He was, however, adapting well and seemed satisfied with his new job as janitor at a local church. How long was she going to be able to keep up this charade? She had twice discouraged the idea of them coming to Dayton to visit her and Laura.

Her problem was partly solved the previous year, but not the way Doris might have liked, when her father had a massive stroke. From her mother's phone call, the indication was that Doris and Laura might not be able to get there in time, but they should come right away. His left side was completely paralyzed, his speech all but impossible to decipher. The only way to communicate was to repeat what they thought he was trying to say. Then try again until one of them said what it was he was trying to tell them, a few grunts, as his eyes brightened up, told them they had it right. Now, a year later, he was really no better, and the toll on Mrs. Aimes was starting to show. Who knew how much longer it might go on?

There were two other people that knew the picture presented by this new man Doris had found was not quite the way it was being told. There were Doris' sister Laura and her husband Ben. When they had asked for Ben's help in withdrawing the court order to garnishee wages, his interest was triggered into action. The story of the computer mix-up was too unlikely to be accepted. No two people

168

were ever issued the same Social Security number. If somehow a wrong number *had* been entered, it was a mistake that could, and should, be corrected. No, it was far more likely that this fellow they called John had somehow taken Jack's identity, with full knowledge of what he was doing.

Ben and Laura had many lengthy discussions about it. Did they as responsible citizens have a duty to bring the matter to the attention of the proper authorities? Still, when they saw how happy Doris was now, and thought about those last miserable years she had spent with Jack, they decided they would not shake any trees or rock any boats. Just let life go on. Doris and her new man could carry on as the loving family they appeared to be.

Chapter 29

Dayton, Ohio, Three Years Later

One evening after the children were in bed, Doris was ironing clothes. It was the commercial on the TV that made her smile. It was a cat food ad, there were about five cats pushing each other out of the way to get at a bowl of the stuff. Ginger, the household pet, was sitting on a footstool and really seemed to be watching. Doris on many occasions had told John, as she knew him, about the cat lady and how they had acquired Ginger. As she tried to get his attention now, she might as well have been talking to a wall. He was in another world, as he read the evening paper.

Very little Canadian news ever made it into the American media, but the local paper often had a column on the third page headed "World News." Tonight there were a few items from Canada. Harry skipped over whatever Brian Mulroney had said, and he barely saw the item about a transit strike in Vancouver. The next item he read and reread.

"A long outstanding murder case in Saskatchewan has been solved. Marvin Harley (Bud) Soelen in a plea bargain, pleaded guilty to manslaughter in the beating death of Lucille Lavina Welks of Tudor, Saskatchewan, and was sentenced to ten years in prison." There was not a word about the missing Harry Welks, and not a word about Irma Soelen.

When Doris saw the disturbed look on Harry's face she said, "John, is something wrong? You look as if you have just seen a ghost." Harry showed her the news item and then went on to tell her the full story of his past. He omitted nothing. The tragic death of his parents, the thing about Lucille, the affair with Irma, the escape, the death and burial of Jack Nelson. It was getting late when he finished, but

170

Harry felt a great weight was lifted from his shoulders. At the end of the narrative Doris said, "I always knew you kept a part of your past hidden, but I also knew you would tell me about it when the time was right.

"Now that your name has been cleared, will you go back to Canada and take up where you left off with Irma?" Doris held her breath awaiting Harry's answer.

"No, Doris, if you and the children want me, I would like to carry on just the way we are, I feel that I have finally come home. Irma was a nice person, she has likely found someone else by now. She was very outgoing and made friends easily."

Doris wasn't long in answering, "Of course we want you to stay, the children love you and we've never been so happy. As far as Jack goes, I felt in my heart he must be dead. He was in very poor heath due to the drug and alcohol abuse. To be honest, he didn't die that night in the house in Bismark, not really, I lost him in Vietnam," she shrugged. "Actually it would have been better, if he had lost his life in combat. At least then his name would be on a scroll somewhere with the names of all the other brave American men and women who gave their lives for their country. Or whatever it was they were over there for."

"Ah! But then fate would never have brought us together," replied Harry. "It is so strange, the way a quirk of fate can change the path of a person's life."

Harry did suggest that when Jack was rambling in his delirium, he may have been remembering their early days of marriage. Doris hoped so, they had been happy back then. Then she suggested that Harry write to Irma, to put her mind at ease. Irma just might still be looking forward to Harry's return someday.

Harry said, "Suppose she took the letter to the police and they come after me for escaping custody. Besides if this country found out that I was an illegal alien that had accepted employment under an alias, the justice system here might be a bit disturbed. Not reporting a death and disrespect for the dead could be something else that would be looked into." They agreed not to take the chance. It would be better to wait, and write his letter the next summer. What difference would a few more months make! They had already started making arrangements for a trip to Disneyland for their holidays. Harry would mail a letter to Irma from somewhere in California.

He would tell her he had met and married a wonderful woman. They had two children, he would not mention the children's ages or who their father was. He would tell her they were living under an assumed name, their home was in San Diego, where they both worked. He would tell her that he had read about Bud having been convicted in the matter of Lucille's death. Still, even though his name may have been cleared of that crime, he and his new wife had too much to lose to reveal himself now. He'd need to let her know that he would never be returning to Canada. Tell her that she was a good person that deserved more out of life than she'd been getting. He would wish her well and give closure to that chapter of his life.

He would give no return address, and when they talked about the little lie regarding San Diego, Harry said he had been living a lie for over three years, so another one for the good of their relationship wouldn't do any harm.

Doris told him that mentioning being married again was also a bit of a lie. "Well! We could correct that," replied Harry, "Next summer, when we go to Disneyland, we could stop in Las Vegas. I have heard there is a chapel there that will perform marriages on the spot. If we use the same names as we are using now, the record will only show a renewal of vows. But for us it will be an important milestone in our lives."

With that Harry got on his knees in front of Doris and asked her to be his wife. She accepted without hesitation, but she never told any of her friends what the new diamond on her left hand meant.

They also came to another important decision that night. That dream home in the suburbs, might now became a reality. It was much like the one that Jack and Doris had visualized in their minds, as they planned the house with a two car garage, back in those promising years before Vietnam. There were two years left in the life of the mortgage on the acreage at Bismark, but there was a clause in it that said they could pay it off at any time. With more than enough in their joint bank account to clear up the mortgage, it would not take long to secure a clear title. When advertised for sale, it would no doubt bring double the money that Jack and Doris had paid old Uncle Andrew for it in the first place. It will be remembered that the good uncle had put it up for sale in the dead of winter.

Doris and hubby would wait until spring, when the grass was greening up, before they put it on the market. While these plans took place, Doris wondered if the mice would have reestablished themselves after the long vacancy. She told Harry, or "John Henry," the name she had hit on as fitting for the man who would share the rest of her life, that they should go out and check on the buildings, at least to give the house a good cleaning if nothing else. With the walls now gyprock, with rock wool insulation, it would not be a playground for mice as it had been with the beaver-board and wood shavings. The mice might, however, be enjoying the cellar and attic. If so they should hire a exterminator to get rid of the pests.

It would likely be a good idea to have electrical service reinstated as well. Yes, if they handled it right the proceeds from the sale would give them enough for a good down payment on the house they already had their eye on.

They finally went to bed, but were still too keyed up to sleep. On thinking over the story he had told Doris, Harry remarked he had lived more than a lifetime in the last few years, and fate had surely caused more than a few turns in the pathway of his life.

Doris said, "Darling, you should write a book, just change the names of the characters and call it fictional." Harry laughed, "We'll see." Doris told Harry she could do the part about Jack growing up in Williston. She still had the clippings she had gleaned from the newspapers during the Vietnam War. She thought if they used their imagination and the newspaper clippings they could write about what Jack's life might have been like in Vietnam. "What the heck, if it strays from the truth, the book would be fictional anyway," they both agreed.

Harry said, "Let's take our time with it, we will each write a bit whenever we have time. Then when we are done we will feed it into a computer and sort it into chapters." Doris said, "I'll bet Laura's husband, Ben, would be willing to edit our book. He reads a lot and is good with words. He could rephrase it where needed, and would know where to end the chapters, so that the reader's attention would be held throughout the story." They agreed that even if they didn't produce a best seller, or even get it published for that matter, it would be fun to do and therapeutic for them both.

So it was decided, they would write a book and entitle it *What Destiny, Oh Path of Fate.*

With that they kissed goodnight before going to sleep.

But it was only Harry that fell asleep, it was almost daylight before Doris dropped off for a while. The fantastic drama that had unfolded kept running through her mind, over and over. Such a strange story, it was hard to believe, especially as she realized that she was part of it.

Chapter 30

Dayton, Ohio

Morning finally came, and Harry got up and made coffee as he always did. It being Saturday, they did not have to get the children up, nor did they have to go to work themselves. Even though it had been a sleepless night, Doris was up and about by eight o'clock.

"John," she said, "I did some more thinking after you went to sleep."

"About what?" said Harry. "About what we will be writing in our book, anyone reading it will want to know what became of the character Irma. I'd like to meet her myself, she sounds like a nice person. Suppose we took a trip to Moose Jaw, and went to the café where you said she worked. If she was still there I would try and get her into a conversation by asking about the Frank Welks family. We'd have to make up some kind of a story as to why I was interested. Perhaps, would tell her my father knew a Frank Welks in the army that came from somewhere around Moose Jaw. There is no need to tell her I am an American, nor is there any reason that the name Nelson would arouse any suspicions when I introduce myself."

Harry listened to her and thought for awhile, then said, "Well, I hope you weren't planning to have me with you when you meet Irma. Besides, why cover the fact that you are an American, and raise the name Welks so soon in the conversation? We should think about it for awhile. How about this for an idea—there are lots of guided bus tours into Canada, good ones. Let's say we got one that went from here to Winnipeg, then went west to Calgary with an overnight stop in Moose Jaw. After Calgary and the Calgary Stampede, it would be on to the resort spots, Banff and Lake Louise, then back into the States, and into Montana to see where Custer's Last Stand took place."

Doris said, "Would that be next summer sometime?"

"Yes, that stampede is in July."

"If we did that, we'd have to cancel the Disney trip, and the kids are already looking forward to that," said Doris.

They agreed not to rush into anything too quickly, but to think over the alternatives. Harry said he liked the idea of a bus trip rather than being on their own. Before meeting Irma, Harry would give her the name of one of Irma's former schoolteachers. "Then go on to tell her that the schoolteacher was a cousin, who you had never met. Go on to say, yes, you are with the tour bus, and your husband has taken a side trip to the Air Base. Tell her he's always been interested in aviation, and since you weren't, you decided to see if you could find any trace of the cousin. If Irma is there she would be sure to notice the children, and start talking to them about their trip. This would give Doris the chance to ask her if she had children of her own, then play it by ear. There might be lots of information to come out of meeting Irma."

As Harry went on thinking out loud, the next suggestion seemed like a gem, when he said, "Once you get her engaged in conversation, start telling her how fascinated you've been with Moose Jaw. Having lived most of your life in Williston, a town that is only a three hour drive away, you've often heard about the place, but this is the first time you've ever been here. Hint at a few of the tales you've read, say something about Al Capone, and there will be a few others as we put a dialog together. Then if it's going well mention a case you read about just a few years ago, some guy murdering his wife in a little town near here, but he escaped from a police car and got away by grabbing a freight train. Tell her you never read whether the fellow ever got caught or not. Then say he probably did, as it seems to me your police force has a motto, something about, 'the Mounties always get their man.' "

Doris said, "It sounds like I might be having an interesting and informative visit with Irma. Another thing I've been thinking about is finding a nice name for Irma. As the names of the characters are to be changed, to make our story a work of fiction, I'd like to make an Irish colleen out of her. Maybe we could call her Colleen. Jack's Aunt Mary was Irish, and he sure thought she was nice. He liked to

176

talk about that summer holiday he spent there, and the great cookies she made."

"Sounds okay," said Harry, "and how about O'Leary for a last name. We could make her a descendant of that woman who owned the cow that kicked over the lantern that started the great Chicago fire."

"Is there a local paper that you could search the back copies of, while I visit Irma. . . . I mean Colleen?" said Doris. "Oh, yes," replied Harry, "*The Moose Jaw Times,* and it has back copies on microfilm. You just start a reel and when it gets to the news item you want to read about, you bring it to a stop."

Harry then told her that without doing any research, he could come pretty close to guessing as to how they got a confession out of Bud. "He likely got liquored up and bragged to Irma about how he got rid of that showoff Welks. I can just hear him saying, 'I might not have sent him to jail, as I intended, but you can be sure that wherever he's hiding, he's looking over his shoulder and scared shitless every minute of every day. Likely wishes he was in a good safe jail,' and when Irma says, 'Are you saying that you killed Lucille?' He likely replied, 'Yeah, and don't think about going to the police because I will deny saying it. And what's more a wife can't testify against her own husband.' He'd probably go on to tell her that he knew what was going on between her and Welks, so he fixed it so the bastard won't mess with Bud Soelen's wife again."

Harry continued with his version of what had really taken place by saying, "but Irma no doubt did go to the police, and while she would never testify, it gave the police a positive suspect. Then they would break him down with continued questioning and finally plea-bargain for the manslaughter charge. The police would be happy at getting the case closed, even if they never got a first degree murder conviction. Half a loaf would be better than none."

"Okay," said Doris, "we'll work your version of that segment into our story. Then we need to plan an end for it. Though before we do that let's think about plans for our own life, that will not be fiction. For starters, you will have to convince the children that it will be more fun to see those majestic and beautiful Canadian Rockies than it would be to go to Disneyland next summer. That shouldn't be much

177

trouble for you though, as they accept anything you tell them as gospel, especially Bobby."

Doris continued, "We are going to have to tell Ben and Laura the truth, if we're going to get Ben to edit our book. They already know that the computer story is a made-up yarn. Laura has hinted that to me on more than one occasion, especially when I needed her as a confident, in making up the story of Jack being employed as a church janitor. Then I had to get her to promise that she would never tell our parents that you were not the real Jack Nelson.

"We will have to let Mother know the full story too, so you can meet her. You will like her, and I know she will be glad to have you as part of the family. I am not sure how Dad would have seen our situation, had he not had that stroke. He was such a stickler for having everything done right. He'd probably insist on you making a clean confession of your past, and facing a court's decision. Oh, he'd likely have put up the money, and seen that you got the best legal advice possible. While I'm not happy with the condition he's in, it has been another 'quirk of fate' that may have made our path a bit smoother."

"I will write to Mother, and tell it all. Then maybe she could come for a visit, a well deserved break, and if she won't have Dad put in a care home, she could at least hire someone to care for him for a week or so. The first line in my letter to Mom will read, 'I hope you are sitting down to read this.'"

"If we are going to postpone the Disney trip for another year or more, you'll need some other way to get a letter to Irma," said Doris.

"Maybe it won't make any difference if I just mail it from here," said Harry.

Doris thought a bit and then said, "Laura told me that Ben is going to Cleveland next week, something about one of his clients, you could sent it with him to mail from there. That's about three hours from here, so no one would make a connection that would lead them to Dayton. Just change your story a bit, this time have us living in Boston, and say we are fans of the Red Sox. We have gone to cheer as they play the Cleveland Indians."

Doris was not through yet. She raised the subject of their marriage and said, "There is another thing that the cancellation of the Disney trip is going to change. When and where are we to have our wedding? I don't know that I could have liked some chapel in Las Vegas anyway. I would like a proper wedding with a real pastor officiating in a real church."

"I'd sure have no problem with that," replied Harry, "you just pick the time and place."

"Well, as long as it won't make you feel uncomfortable, I would like to go back to the church in Williston that Jack and I were married in. It would seem more logical, since for the record it will be a renewal of vows. Mother told me there is a different pastor there now, so looking a bit different from the first Jack Nelson won't matter. I am sure Laura and Ben would go along and stand up with us, the only other person that need be there would be Mother. She'll want the wedding to take place as soon as possible once she knows the facts."

Plans for their own future, as well as their plans of writing a novel, came to a halt as the children got up and wanted breakfast. The day went as most Saturdays did, do some house cleaning in the morning while the kids watched cartoons, then shop for groceries after lunch. Harry played catch with Bobby for awhile before supper. Doris started the letter to her Mother while supper was cooking, though she knew she would likely rewrite it two or three times.

With supper out of the way, and Doris still in the process of rewriting the letter to her Mother, Harry started thinking a bit more about the letter he had planned to send to Irma. The more he thought about it, the idea of writing to her at all was probably not the smartest thing he could do. Already they were going to indicate they were living in Boston, instead of San Diego. My, how easy it was to move in the world of imagination.

Instead of Irma, he would write to his sister Mildred. She would be just as worried about him as Irma, let Irma find out through second hand information. Just tell Mildred it would be okay with him if she were to let some of his friends at Tudor know he was doing well, Jake Meyer in particular. Irma might feel slighted at being left out, but it would likely be the best way to let her know that anything they had between them was over.

Here is a copy of the letter that he sent to Mildred. It was lucky he could remember her address.

Boston, Mass.
Oct 28/79

My dearest sister Mildred,

Hearing from me will no doubt come as a shock to you. After reading a news article that cleared my name of the murder charge I was accused of, I felt I should let you know that life has been very kind to me since boarding that train as it passed under the bridge on Highway One. You have likely heard about that part of it. Little did I think those stories Dad used to tell us of his days as a railroad bum could be put to good use.

Other than letting you know that my life can now be described as a bed of roses, I will not go into very much detail. I often compare my situation today, with those miserable years I spent with Lucille, and it makes me want to go and shake hands with Bud Soelen for the change he made in the path of my life.

I never got to be a chartered accountant as I would have liked, but I am employed by an accounting firm in Boston. I am married to a wonderful woman and we have two lovable children, a boy and a girl. Does your little Anne have a brother or a sister yet? I hope so, and would like to meet them, just as I wish you could meet my family, but I am afraid that day is a long ways into the future, as I have no plans to return to Canada even though my name has been cleared.

I suppose any assets that I had in Tudor are now lost, but if there is any item that could still be salvaged I would like you to have it. I would give you Power of Attorney if I could, perhaps this letter might be accepted as an instrument for that purpose. You once said you would like to see the house kept in the family, but it has likely been taken by the village for non-payment of taxes. Maybe you could buy it from them, as it's not likely to bring much on the auction block. Then there is the car, if it hasn't been completely vandalized it might be worth seven or eight hundred dollars. The piano that Mother used to entertain us with is probably worth more than the car. Remember the good years we had growing up, when Mom played and we all tried to sing. I've often thought she missed her calling. If the piano is still there it would need tuning after such a long time without use. Certainly Lucille never showed any interest in it.

We are great fans of the Boston Red Sox, and as they are going to Cleveland next weekend to play the Indians, we have bought a package that gets us into three games, plus hotel accommodation, and bus fare. We hope the weather is good, as we are so looking forward to this holiday.

If you would like to pass this information on to our friends back in Tudor, Jake Meyer in particular, it will be fine with me. I am sure some are wondering what became of me.

I remain, as always, your ever loving brother Harry.

P.S. Needless to say I no longer use the name Henry (Harry) Alfred Welks, not that I am ashamed of it, but it just seemed to make sense to use another name.

With that done Harry sealed his letter, addressed it correctly, affixed the correct postage for out of country mailing, and left it to be handed to Ben for mailing in Cleveland.

When they were in bed that night, they again started to talk about their novel, how it would start. Doris wanted to tell about how hard Jack had worked, with her at his side doing all she could. Harry thought that should be okay, but they needed to be cautious about giving too much detail. Harry said, "There's lots of books on the market that go on and on about the color of the wallpaper, which way the chairs faced, which way the door opened, and so on. Just a lot of words that have nothing to do with the story content."

"Okay," said Doris, "then we won't mention how much I did while

Jack was in Nam, but I was quite pleased with my efforts, as I painted all the rooms. I thought they looked really good, once I had the kitchen in yellow, the bedroom a pale blue, and the front room an off-white. I was glad that Jack had put the finishing strips around the windows and doors on that brief leave before he went overseas. Because of that I was able to buy and put up curtains, but we won't write anything about it.

"While we are talking about what should not be written," added Doris, "there is another topic I hope we can leave out, and that's page after page of smutty sex. When I get a book like that I skip all those pages, or sometimes just throw the thing away. If the sex act must be mentioned, the details should be left out, leaving that part to the imagination of the reader."

Then on that same subject she said, "There'll be couple of juicy tidbits in your story. Won't there, lover boy. That night in the back seat with Lucille, and the afternoon in the motel with Irma. Which one was best?"

Harry was glad it was dark. She couldn't see his face. After a few moments he said, "Oh, come on. You don't expect me to make those kind of comparisons. In the first place there needs to be an association of love. It certainly wasn't love with Lucille, so it was more like a rutting boar. Irma. Well, as I think back, there may not have been the love I thought, just a means of escape. Further to that, when I thought of Bud Soelen having been there first, the idea became much less appealing. Try as I might to get the big oaf out of my mind, his image was always there.

"No, dear, the first real gentle wonderful love of my life was that first time with you. So sweet, so intoxicating, no previous experience could equal the fervor of that first time we shared our love. Before I came to your bed, I used to lay awake and wonder if there was a possibility of it happening. I would think up words I might use to raise the subject, but nothing ever seemed quite right."

"Too bad you didn't find the right words, because you could have come sooner if you'd wanted to," said Doris.

To which Harry replied, "I would have if you'd have sent an invitation sooner."

182

"But if I'd have done that you might have seen me as a brazen and bold hussy like Lucille," responded Doris.

"By the way," said Harry, "Since we are making comparisons, you've had two men in your life, how do they relate to one another."

"Nothing doing," said Doris, "you won't get me into that, I did love Jack, but in the short time we had together before Vietnam, we worked too hard to be very enthusiastic about anything else, and after Nam. Well! I'd rather not think about it."

It wasn't long until Harry fell asleep, while Doris did think of the men in her life and how the cruel turns and twists of fate had determined the final destiny in the life of Jack Nelson. Even as a child he'd had to fight an uphill battle. Really, as she thought about it she realized that Jack had never been a child. It wasn't fair to compare him with John Henry, the name she had decided would be fitting for the man that now shared her life, but she couldn't help wonder if Jack could have been the kind of father to the children that Harry was, even if there had never been a Nam. Jack knew how to work, but had never learned how to play.

Epilogue

Jake Mayer had regretted his hasty action in calling the police when he first found out about the murder. Shortly after Harry made his getaway, Jake had talked to Irma, and on hearing her story was sure that Harry was not guilty. If he'd gone and talked to Harry before he phoned the police, Harry might have told the truth as to where he was on that fatal afternoon and would never have been arrested.

Harry's letter to Mildred, following so closely on the heels of Bud's confession and prison sentence, caused quite a stir among the residents of Tudor and the surrounding area.

A decision was made to hold a Harry Welks recognition night in the hall in Tudor. It was well advertised, so a large crowd was on hand, including Mildred, her daughter Anne, now twelve years old, and her young son Harry, now two. Anne was more like a mother than a sister to little Harry. A committee was set up and an award called "The Citizen of the Decade" was created to be presented to Mildred on Harry's behalf. This was a bronze plaque set in a nice frame, and had an outline of the many contributions Harry had made to the community engraved on it. The plaque would grace the front wall of the Tudor hall till the end of time.

The Tudor home, as Harry had predicted, had been seized by the village and was now for sale. While Mildred appreciated being able to go through the old place again, she didn't want to buy it. If she did she would have to try and rent it out. Jake Meyer's son, Jake Junior, now twenty-three years old and about to be married, was happy to make a bid on it that was accepted by the village council. Jake Junior assured Mildred that she would be welcome to visit the old house anytime.

With police permission Jake Senior had moved the car to his shed shortly after Harry disappeared. As it was still there the decision was made that Jake Junior would buy it. They would have it appraised at a garage in Moose Jaw. They found out he could licence it in his name on the strength of Harry's letter. Mildred didn't really feel she should take the money, but finally agreed to put it in a savings account for little Harry, his uncle's namesake. If left undisturbed till he was ready for university, the accumulated interest plus the principal would make a worthwhile contribution toward the cost of college. Perhaps he might one day become a chartered accountant, the career that had been denied his uncle.

Jake Junior was glad to get the car as he had a forty hour a week job in Moose Jaw, and by living in Tudor, he could help on his dad's farm on his time off. That would be weekends, statutory holidays, and regular holidays.

Mildred thought she would like the piano, as Anne was showing some interest in music, but how to get it to Barrie, Ontario? Her husband Bob solved that one when he found an old acquaintance at the Airbase that was just being posted to the base at Barrie. The Air Force would pay for moving all his goods and chattels, so it was just a matter of adding the piano to the lot, and off went the piano, courtesy of the Canadian taxpayers. A generous lot, those taxpayers.

Harry had hit the nail right on the head when he told Doris about how Bud came to confess to the murder. Liquored up, one night he had bragged about how he got rid of Welks. When Irma took the story to the police, it was none other than Steven Stenowski that heard her story, the same cop that had been in charge the night of Harry's escape. Irma had met him many times during the investigation, so she was pleased to be able to bring him something that could exonerate Harry. It was Stenowski that had sat with Bud in a little cubicle for three hours without a break, and finally sweated a confession out of him.

Of late Steve, as Irma now called him, was a frequent customer at the café where she still worked. They often discussed what might have been, but for a "quirk of fate" that had allowed Harry to escape that night. If that had not happened and Harry had been brought to trial, would the justice system have exonerated him? Would the court have believed Irma? If he had been sent to jail would Harry have been launching legal action against the system for false imprisonment? Would the courts have ended up having to pay him a bundle of money? That is, if Bud had still done his bragging to Irma, thus establishing Harry's innocence?

Steve had lost his wife a few months ago after a lengthy battle with cancer. She was at last relieved of her suffering at the tender age of forty-five. With his many visits to the café, they were finding out that they had a good deal more in common than just the Harry Welks case. They were both avid sports fans, and were both interested in travel. Irma had got a taste of travel while she was with the Roughrider Dream Team, and she enjoyed it very much. Steve had also seen quite a bit of Canada as a result of various postings with the police force. He told Irma he was sure she would enjoy Alaska, said it must be a lot like the Yukon, the place of his first posting. Those long summer nights were just wonderful. It was on an outing to a football game that Steve asked her to be his wife, and even though he was twenty years her senior, she readily accepted. Her divorce from Bud should be finalized before spring, as he was not contesting it. They planned the wedding for the next July, and for a honeymoon they would go to the British Isles and then on to Poland, the homeland of Steve's parents.

Trips to places like Alaska or the Maritimes, would come later. Steve would retire from the police force in two years, and then they might buy a motor-home. And as they planned it all, they still pondered the "what if's" that brought about the twists in their paths of fate, and changed their destiny.

Harry and Doris are still working on their novel. They had made arrangements for a Canadian tour as soon as school was out next June. There would be an overnight stop in Moose Jaw, but no definite plans were set up as to what they would do when there. Irma might still be employed at the café, but might not be there as she takes a lot of days off now. If Doris misses her it won't make much difference, as all the rest of the staff are well versed in regard to the drama that the John Nelson family, or John Henry as Doris was now becoming comfortable with, are interested in.

◆ ◆ ◆

Watch for *The Hand of Fate,* a sequel to *Quirk of Fate,* expected to be in print soon.

After a stormy marriage breakup, Di finished business school with a class one certificate as a business stenographer.

It took a week or better of scanning ads, making calls, both via phone and in person. Her efforts only resulted in discouraging refusals. Finally, she saw an ad from a clinic needing a secretary; that looked promising. She would make the call in person, so after writing down the address, it was into her little car, and she was on her way.

She soon found out that it was not the type of clinic that she expected. The receptionist was young and very pleasant as she made Di welcome, telling her she had no need to be afraid there. "You've come to the right place," said the receptionist, "we all make these little mistakes, don't we. But it's a mistake that it only takes a few minutes to correct, then we can get on with our lives. Now we need to have you fill out this form, just a few simple questions, the date of your last menstruation period, the name of the father, your age, and so on, there's really nothing to it."

Di was almost speechless, and not at all sure she wanted to work at an abortion clinic. However she did need a job, so she said to the lady, "No, no! I'm not here for what you think. I came in response to your ad saying there is an opening for a secretary." Di could feel a big drop in the temperature, as the receptionist said, "Oh! well you will need to talk to the matron about that, however she's not in today, but if you'd like to drop back tomorrow you will be able to see her."

Di gave the events of the afternoon a lot of consideration that evening, as well as most of the night. Could she bring herself to work in a place like that, she pondered. Really until now, the subject of abortion had rarely, if ever, crossed her mind. If she had an opinion at all, whether having an abortion was something to be decided by the woman, the man involved, her doctor, and perhaps her pastor, *certainly not the politicians.* Anyway she needed a job, and if it didn't go well, perhaps something else would turn up later.

The interview went fine, she was immediately given a desk and went to work. For the most part, for the next six months, it was a paying job, and she was content. The "right-to-life activists" gave them some harassment as they arrived or left the clinic, but for the most part the police were able to keep them at bay.

Robert, still looking for a cause of some kind of support, saw the abortion debate as a hot topic. There was money to be made there, if he handled himself right. At first glance he wasn't sure which action group he would come out in support of. Would it be the "right-to-life" gang or would it be the "pro-choicers." He finally settled for the "pro-choicers," as there seemed to be more of them, at least they were the most vocal. He knew Di worked there, and in no way would he do anything to hurt her, but by being in the thick of it he might even be able to protect her. Tell her what days to phone in sick, and so on.

Very little consideration was given to the bible or to religious teachings in the Nelson home. It was Doris' idea and desire that resulted in her marriage to Harry taking place in a church with a pastor officiating, *Harry would have been just as satisfied, had they have taken their vows before a Justice of the Peace.* And it was at Doris' insistence that they attended church on Easter Sunday on each year. It was therefore not surprising that neither of the children had much of a grasp on the subject of theology.

Robert soon found out that he would get passages from the bible thrown at him by the "right-to-life" group. Abortion was murder, they said, as they found some scripture to quote, including the Sixth Commandment that says "Thou Shalt Not Kill."

He would have to bone up on the Bible. One of the activists was from out of town, and had a room in a local motel. It was in the room of his friend that Robert took his first serious look at a Bible, the one left by the Gideons. He knew he could never read it all or find any scripture that might be of some use to him. His friend, however, had been made to attend Sunday school as a child. Then later he filled a church pew on a regular basis.

They spent an evening looking up passages that could be used to support their cause, while the friend assured him that abortion was not mentioned anywhere in the Bible as being right or wrong. Robert guessed the word hadn't been invented when the Bible was written. They did, however, find a number of passages that defined life as breath, therefore there could be no life until a baby left its mother's womb and started to breathe on its own. An example of this was found in the story of Adam's creation, in Genesis 2:7 when God "breathed into his nostrils the breath of life; and man became a living soul." So if life didn't start until breathing took place, how could aborting a fetus be considered killing?

Like all the other causes that Robert had taken up and sounded the trumpet for, he soon had a convincing vocabulary that proved "it was a woman's right to do as she wished with her own body." Not only could he get the attention of crowds with his bullhorn, but he was soon getting invited as a guest on radio talk shows.

He made a point of never being sarcastic or abusive with a caller, even though some had used remarks that might even be considered libel.

A dialog might go as follows.

CALLER: Where would you be now, if your mother had of aborted you, do you ever think of that?

ROBERT, IN HIS SMOOTH GENTLE VOICE: Well, obviously I wouldn't be here now, would I, but then if my mother would have had a headache the night I was conceived, I wouldn't be here either. You know, getting born is just a chance thing, but, caller, may I ask you if you have children?

CALLER: Oh, yes, I have two that I'm very proud of and never once thought of aborting either of them.

ROBERT: I'm sure you didn't, but tell me, how old are your children?

CALLER: One is ten and the youngest is six.

ROBERT: My, but you sound young to have a child that's ten years old.

CALLER: I'll have you know I was twenty-two years old when Sally came to us, and twenty-six when Arnold arrived.

ROBERT: A lovely family for sure, but at that age, you surely could have had a much larger family than two, why weren't there more?

CALLER: My husband and I discussed it and felt that two was just right, so we practiced family planning.

ROBERT: Ah, yes, a wonderful idea, and I guess what you really mean by family planning could be called birth control.

CALLER: I suppose so, but I don't see what it has to do with abortion.

ROBERT: Nothing perhaps, but don't you agree that your practice of birth control, or family planning as you call it, has denied at least a few children of a right to life? Children that could have been born into a happy home, with an abundance of warmth and love. Children that might have taken their place in society, and perhaps made the world a better place for us all. Perhaps the children that you have denied a right to life, would have had a much fuller life than a child that is being born to a mother that already has ten kids that she can't look after, but can't terminate her pregnancy because someone says it's against the will of God.

Callers usually came up with some quote from the Bible. Robert would then ask the caller if he or she believed everything in the Bible, and if the caller answered, "Yes," he would read off a scripture that suited him. His favorite was Genesis 3:16. "I will greatly multiply thy sorrow and thy conception, in sorrow thy shalt bring forth children; and thy desire shall be to thy husband, and he shall rule over thee." Then he'd suggest that no woman today would agree with anything like that.

Yes, Robert was even starting to believe his own stuff, for the first time since he started joining the various protest groups. He was even starting to feel good about the side he had taken on the question of abortion. But more important was the size of the donations to the cause that continued to roll in.

It all came to a sad ending though, ironically it happened on Robert's birthday December 23. What a birthday present, and what a way to spend Christmas. One of the protesters, (or was it?) manufactured a bomb. Just a piece of plastic pipe, filled with explosives and a blasting cap, one wire was clamped into the cap, while a second wire was taped to the cap's metal body. The device was then hung on the frame on the underside of Di's car. The culprit had to know what he was doing when he opened the harness containing the car's electrical wiring. The bomb was not fitted to a wire that would feed the car's ignition switch. No, it was fitted to wires that would activate the explosive device as soon as the lights were turned on. As the parking lot was well lighted, Dianne would not be expected to turn the lights on until she was leaving the lot, but before pulling onto the road.

It went just as planned, Dianne was killed instantly, with no other vehicles involved. It took a long and extensive investigation, but it was finally revealed that the culprit was not a "pro-choicer" but a "right-to-life" activist. It was also found out that the target was not Di, but Robert. The villain knew how Robert felt about his sister, and here was the perfect method of hurting him.

Not only was Robert hurt, but so was the entire Nelson family and all their friends. Doris had a nervous breakdown, and spent the next year undergoing psychiatric treatment. If any good came out of it, it was that Robert and his father were brought back together. They actually cried as they went into each others' arms.